A KISS at MISTLETOE

KISS THE WALLFLOWER, BOOK 2

TAMARA Gill

COPYRIGHT

A Kiss at Mistletoe
Kiss the Wallflower, Book 2
Copyright © 2019 by Tamara Gill
Cover Art by Wicked Smart Designs
Editor Author Designs
All rights reserved.

ISBN-13: 978-0-6487160-0-6
ISBN-10: 0-6487160-0-7

DEDICATION

For those who love to kiss under the mistletoe.

CHAPTER 1

*L*ady Mary Dalton, eldest daughter to the Earl of Lancaster jiggled her fishing pole, having felt a rapid jerk of her line. Too slow to catch the fish, she left her line in the water hoping to feel another little nibble and possibly reel in a nice-sized carp or bream for Cook to prepare for dinner tomorrow.

The snow relentlessly fell outside as she sat wrapped up in furs and wool on the family's frozen lake in Derbyshire. The ice house her father had the servants move onto the lake each year was a welcome retreat from her mother's complaints. Mama didn't think ladies should fish, particularly in the middle of winter. Women should be wives. Women should have husbands. Women should have children. Her daughter should be married by now...

Blah, blah, blah, she'd heard the words too many times to count.

It was practically the countess's motto. Unfortunately, what her mama wished for was the opposite of what Mary wanted. She'd never been like her friends, had never loved shopping in London in the weeks leading up to their first

Season. She cared very little if the men of the *ton* thought her a worthy, profitable or pretty ornament for their arm.

The outdoors had always been her passion and some days she'd wished she'd been born a man, or even into a family that were not titled and rich. Just an ordinary, working family that could do as they pleased. At least, that was what she'd always thought everyone else had since her own life had been so orchestrated.

Mary jiggled her line a little and sighed. At least she was home at present, thanks to her mama falling ill with a cold that she could not possibly stay in Town to endure since someone might see her red nose.

With any luck, her mother would decide to stay in Derbyshire and not travel back to Town to finish up the Little Season before Christmas. Thankfully, spring and summer would soon return and she was looking forward to those months. When the snow melted away and rivers ran and she was able to go outdoors again not just to fish on the ice but to walk the surrounding hills and forests and climb the rocky outcrops that scattered her magnificent county.

The door to the icebox opened and her father entered. He was rugged up in a fur coat, a hood covered his head and most of his brow. A thick woolen scarf wrapped about his mouth and nose, and he looked like an Eskimo. Mary chuckled as he came in and shut the door, before sitting on the little wooden stool across from her. He picked up the spare fishing rod, placing bait on the small hook and dropped the line into the water, dangling it just as she had.

"Mary, there is something we need to discuss, my dear," he said.

His downcast tone didn't bode well for them to remain in the country and she prepared herself for the disappointing news that was undoubtedly to come.

"My dearest girl is to be three and twenty in few days, and

it is time for us to have you settled and married before the end of the next Season. We thought our annual Mistletoe Ball would be the perfect opportunity to invite our neighbors and their guests to celebrate Yuletide. It would also act as a reintroduction for you into society and to show those present that you're most definitely seeking a husband next year and are open to courtship."

The thought sent revulsion through her and she stared at her father a moment, wondering if he'd lost his mind. It was one thing to return to London, but using their Christmas ball as a means to showcase her assets was mortifying. "Must we go back to London at all? You know I do not do well in Town. I am not like the other girls. I don't take pleasure in grand balls and parties. I'm much more comfortable here in my ice fishing box, swimming in our lake or walking the beautiful park with Louise. I'll be miserable if you make me endure another Season. Even you said how much you loathe London and the backstabbing *ton* who live there."

Her father half laughed, jiggling his line. "You're right I do abhor it, but you need a husband, to be given a secure future and happy marriage. Just as your mama and I have had."

That was true, her parents had a very happy and loving relationship, but that didn't mean such a path was the one she wanted to tread. What was wrong with being a wallflower that wilted into an old, unmarried maid? Nothing in Mary's estimation. To be married meant she would have to conform to society, be a lady all the time, host teas and balls. Live in Town most of the year and submit to a husband's whims. Such a life would not be so bad if she found a man to marry whom she loved, and who loved her. A gentleman who liked the country life over that of London and allowed her the freedom which she was used to. But after numerous failed Seasons already, *that* was unlikely to occur.

Her heart twisted in her chest. "I do not want to return. Please don't make me, Papa."

"We must, but with Christmas upon us, we'll have more time here at Bran Manor, plenty of time for you to enjoy the last few months of being an unmarried woman."

Her father looked at her as if such news would make everything well. It did not.

He cleared his throat. "We want to see you happily married and settled. I would love nothing better than to welcome a titled gentleman, worthy of an earl's daughter into our family. You never know, you may find a man who loves the hobbies that you do, admires and appreciates your exuberance for life and country walks."

Or she might find no one of the kind, make a terrible mistake that she would be stuck with for the rest of her life. "What if I don't find anyone with such qualities, Papa? Last Season, certainly I never did. All the gentlemen were self-absorbed dandies who inspected mirrors more than they interacted with the women surrounding them."

Her father chuckled, tugging sharply on his line and pulling out a good-sized trout.

Mary despaired at the sight of his catch. She'd sat here for hours and hadn't caught a thing and here was her papa, not here five minutes and he'd caught the largest fish she'd seen all winter.

She shook her head at him. "You're no longer invited into my ice hut. You cheat," she said jokingly, smiling at her papa.

He grinned, looking down at his catch. "I'll have Cook prepare this for tomorrow night. It will be a feast."

"You know, Papa, I'm an heiress and financially independent no matter whom I marry, thanks to you, Mama, and Grandmother Lancaster. Why should I marry at all? It's not like the family needs funds, and I will never be considered an old, poor maid not worthy of society's company. Your title and wealth prohibit such ostracism. So is it really necessary that we go? There may be a young man in Derbyshire who is looking for a wife and would be perfect for me. I could have the love of my life right beneath my very nose, and miss him by going to London, looking for the wrong man."

Her father paused from putting the fish in a nearby basket, before he said, "I must remember to give your tutor a better letter of recommendation due to the fact you're able to negotiate and barter as well as those in the House of Lords." Her father threw her a consoling smile. "But, alas, we do not live in a time where young women of means and of family can live independently without a husband. I will not allow you to be placed on a shelf to have dust settle on your head, nor will I allow you to live an unfulfilled life without a husband and children of your own. You would be an asset to anyone's family you married into, and I want to see you happy."

Anger thrummed through her at the narrow-minded idea that she needed a man to make all her dreams come true. She did not need a husband to be happy, and the sooner her father and the men hunting her fortune realized this, the better.

Mary yanked up her fishing line, placing her rod against the wall. "I don't see why I have to marry anybody. This is 1800! A new century, please tell me that gentlemen of society and England will come out of the dark ages and see that women are worth more than what they can bring to a marriage, or how large a dowry they have, or how wide their hips are for breeding!"

Her father raised his brow, clearly shocked. "Hush now! I'll hear no more protest from you. I would never force you into a marriage you did not want with your whole heart. We want you to be happy, to find a gentleman who allows you the freedom to which you've grown accustomed. But you *will* marry, my child, and you will continue to have Seasons in Town until you do."

Mary couldn't believe her father. It was as if he were only half listening to her. "I will not find someone. I know this to be true." She crossed her arms, hating the idea of going back to London. "You know as well as anyone that I'm terrible around people. I get nervous at balls and parties so that I'll say something out of line, or not be fashionable enough. I stutter when asked direct questions, and my face tends to turn a terrible, unflattering shade of red during all those things. Please do not do this to me, Papa. *Please*," she begged him.

Her father stood, seemingly having enough fishing for one day. "You are going and for your mother's sake, you will enjoy the Season or at least make a show of enjoyment while in public. Do not fret, my dear," he said, his tone turning cajoling. "We will be there with you. To hold your hand and not let you fail."

She blinked back the tears that threatened. Her first Season had been miserable. Her mother, even with a fortune at her disposal had not procured her a fashionable modiste and so she'd been dressed in frills and ribbons that made her look like a decoration instead of a debutante. Her gowns had clashed against her olive-toned skin and dark hair and not a lot had improved regarding her wardrobe since that time.

Even despite her father being titled, with multiple properties about England and her dowry being more than anyone could spend in two lifetimes, no one had befriended her or took her under their wing other than her dearest companion Louise, of course. Mary sighed, knowing it was not entirely everyone else's fault that she was ostracized in Town. She'd gone above and beyond to distance herself from girls her own age, and had been cold and aloof to the gentlemen who had paid court to her.

At three and twenty, what was left open to her but to be standoffish. To marry at such a young age would mean her lifestyle, her love of the outdoors and pursuits indulged in only by those of the opposite sex would end. Would have to end because her new husband would demand it of her. Demand she acted as the earl's daughter she was born and as his wife.

Mary met her father's gaze and read the concern in his eyes and a little part of her disobedience crumbled. She hated to disappoint her parents, and of course she wanted them to not worry about her, but how could she marry and remain the woman she was?

She narrowed her eyes, thinking of possibilities. "If I'm being forced to go, Papa, and I do wish to state that I am in no way agreeable about traveling to London. But if I do have to go, smile, dance and play the pretty debutante, there are some rules that I wish to instruct you and Mama of."

Her father stopped adjusting his fur coat and gave her his full attention "What is it that you want, Mary? We're open to negotiation."

"I will choose whom I marry. I will not be swayed otherwise. The man I marry will suit me in all ways and I will not be pressured to choose if one does not materialize next Season." Mary raised her chin, waiting for her father's response, but when he did nothing but stare at her patiently, she continued. "I want a new wardrobe for the Season. And I'd like a lady's maid of my own, not Mama's. She has a habit of putting my hair up in styles like Mother's and it makes me look..." Mary fought for words that wouldn't hurt her father's feelings when discussing his wife.

"A woman of mature years?" he said, smiling a little.

"Yes." She nodded empathically, "That is exactly what I mean."

Her father regarded her for a moment before he came

over to her, placing his arm about her shoulder. "That does not seem like it's too much to ask. I will speak to your mama and ensure she will not stand in your way."

"Thank you, Papa." Mary busied herself putting her gloves on while she pushed down the guilt her request brought forth. Had she wanted to, she could've asked for a new modiste and maid years ago and her parents would never have stood in her way. But her determination to remain an unmarried maid had made her hold her tongue. Being unfashionable in Town had meant very few wished to be around her, or be seen on the dance floor with her, and that had suited her very well. But she could not remain so forever, not if her parents were so determined to see her as a wife. If she had to embark on this side of life, at least it would be under her terms and with any luck she'd find a gentleman who'd enjoy the outdoors as much as she did and not wish to clip her wings. To find such a man she supposed she would have to mingle more and actually bother to get to know them this Season.

"Come, let us get this fish back home. I'm sure the dinner gong will sound very soon."

Mary let her father shuffle her out the door, before they started back toward the house. In the dissipating light, the estate was a beacon of warmth and much preferred than where they currently were. Mary resigned herself to the fact that they would return to London in the spring, but at least she would have control of her gowns and there was Christmas here in Derbyshire to enjoy.

Her elder brother always brought friends to stay, and so this year would be just as merry as every other. A little calm before the storm that was the Season.

CHAPTER 2

November 1800

*D*ale Ramsay, the Duke of Carlton stood to the side of the room, watching the gathering throng in his closest friend, the Viscount Kensley, the future Earl of Lancaster's drawing room waiting for the dinner gong to sound so they could eat.

They had traveled all day, and Dale had to admit that if they did not get some food into him soon, he would either tumble over from too much wine, or his stomach would growl so loudly that the women present would think him a bear.

Mistletoe hung from every possible location in the room, from doorways to the candelabras. Lady Lancaster had even placed little cuttings of it and located them on sideboards, mantles, anywhere there was a spare spot. Was the lady looking for the few young women and men that were here present to steal a kiss or two?

Not that Dale would mind stealing a kiss if one was available. There were certainly some very fetching young women in attendance.

The drawing room door opened and taking a sip of wine, he coughed, choking a little on his drink at the sight he beheld. What a monstrosity, or better yet, who was the young woman who was dressed like someone who'd stepped out of the mid-eighteenth century?

He took out his handkerchief, wiped at his mouth, and watched as Peter went up to the young woman, pulling her into a fierce hug and kissing her soundly on the cheek.

Dale observed the young woman was not completely unfortunate, even though she was wearing spectacles. Was the poor woman also blind? It would certainly explain the lack of knowledge regarding her gown. You could not fix what you could not see.

Peter started toward him and Dale schooled his features to one of polite interest. As his friend neared the young woman, he took in her appearance more. Her dark long locks were tied back into a design that Lady Lancaster also sported, but it did not compliment the young woman. Nor did the mustard-colored gown she suffered to wear since it made her look washed out and even a little ill.

"Carlton, may I introduce to you my sister, Lady Mary. Mary, this is my good friend, the Duke of Carlton."

She bobbed a neat curtsy, and stared up at him with the widest green eyes he'd ever beheld. Her gown was of little advantage and Dale had an overwhelming urge to send her to his ex-mistresses' modiste in London, who was one of the most sought after and finest seamstresses in the city.

Dale bowed slightly. "Lady Mary, it is a pleasure to meet you at last. Your brother has spoken of you often."

She threw him a doubtful look but smiled. She did have a very pretty smile. "I'm sure you lie, your grace, but thank you, in any case. I shall take your charming words and believe them."

Peter chuckled. "Mary, do not tease the duke. He will think you mean what you say."

Her eyes skimmed him from top to toe, and Dale had the oddest sensation run through him. Her inspection wasn't at all what he thought a young unmarried woman ought to do to a peer, and yet this country miss, an earl's daughter no less, whom he'd never met in his life before seemed to think it appropriate.

"Perhaps I do not tease, Brother." She grinned mischievously, and Dale found himself smiling.

He schooled his features once more. "On the contrary, my lady. Your brother has spoken highly of you and I'm pleased to make your acquaintance."

"And I you, your grace." She studied him with shrewd eyes, and he met her boldness by raising his brow. "You spend most of your time in Town I assume?"

"I do," he said, glad she'd stopped inspecting him like an insect that needed stomping on. He was sure that she did not approve his answer.

She glanced about, her disinterest in their conversation obvious. "I dislike London and I'm not looking forward to going back, but alas, as a female I have little choice. Isn't that right, Brother?"

Peter shook his head at his sister. "Mary, let us not quarrel in front of our guests. You know I'm looking forward to having you in Town next year."

She sighed, plucking a glass of wine from a passing footman and taking a sip. "I should imagine you love the Season, your grace? Enjoy the nights out about Town, the horse rides in the park among other things."

Dale clamped his mouth shut. *Other things...* what on earth did that mean? Did she allude to the many gambling hells he attended, nights at Vauxhall or the many women who sought his companionship? He glanced down at her, her fierce green eyes full of mirth stared back without a by-your-leave.

He marveled at her boldness. "I do enjoy all the delicacies that Town affords. So many entertainments to appreciate, it is like one big feast that I cannot get enough of."

Mary's cheeks turned a delightful shade of rose, and he grinned.

Peter cleared his throat. "I see Miss Grant has arrived, Mary."

She glanced behind her and bobbing a quick curtsy excused herself, leaving Dale to watch after her as she joined the woman who looked a similar age to her by the window.

"Is your sister out, Peter?" he asked, watching her still. Now with her friend, Lady Mary seemed to brighten even more when having a conversation with someone she liked.

"She had her coming out five years ago, but nothing came of it or any subsequent Seasons. Our parents are hoping to gain her a match with the forthcoming Season, much to Mary's distaste."

Dale raised his brow, taking a sip of his wine. "Oh, she does not wish for marriage?" It wasn't often any young woman of Lady Mary's age would not want such a thing. Certainly, Dale had never met such a woman before in his life, and he had five years on Mary if he correctly estimated her age.

"How old is your sister?" Dale asked, unable to tear his eyes from her as she moved about the room. The idea that he found the Lady Mary interesting enough to do such a thing pulled him up short and he shifted his gaze from her.

Peter's eyes met his over the top of his wine glass and the steely edge to his friend's gaze gave him pause. "Why so much interest in Mary?"

Dale raised one hand. "I was merely making conversation. I'm not interested in your sister as anything other than a friend. I did not see her in Town last year and was merely curious as to her age." And part of what he said was indeed true, he was curious about the woman who seemed to have a voice, despite that her gown stated otherwise, and she was without fear of him. Being a duke there were few who could boast such a thing. Other than his friend Peter that is.

"Mary has just turned three and twenty." Peter glanced about the room. "Lady Hectorville is here, I see. That should make you happy, Carlton."

Dale fought not to cringe at the mention of the late earl's wife. "Not particularly. I had one liaison with the woman, when I was in my cups and she was hiding her appearance at the time and I did not know it was her."

"Much to her despair. Look, my friend, she is observing you and seems quite forlorn that you have not said hello."

His friend laughed and Dale threw him a quelling glance. "That night was a mistake and one I shall not make again. I have apologized to her, even though she did not want to hear it, but either way, what is done is done and she's since moved on with another of our set."

"Maybe you ought to tell her that she needs to move on from you, because from where I stand it certainly does not seem that way."

Dale looked to where Peter had glanced and he ground his teeth. Damn it, he'd never thought her ladyship would be here of all places. How was it that the woman was even invited? She stood beside Lady Lancaster and her determined interest in Dale must be obvious to any who bothered to notice.

"How is your family acquainted with Lady Hectorville?"

"She is one of my mother's closest friends. They have known each other for many years, even though there is a fifteen-year age gap between them. When they're together you would not know that was the case."

Fabulous, that was all Dale needed. A meddling Lady Hectorville who sometimes still sent him love notes begging for him to call, or Peter's mother who undoubtedly knew he'd tumbled one of her closest friends. He cringed.

"So, my friend, what are we going to do now that I have you up here in Derbyshire. We may go riding tomorrow if you like. There are some very fine locations to visit about the property, and I wish to show you the hunting lodge. Could be a thought to bring up a group of friends in the summer and make use of it. What say you?"

Dale lifted his wine glass in mock salute. "I think that sounds like a wonderful idea on both counts. Shall we say we'll meet at the stables at nine in the morning to scout it out?"

Peter clinked his glass against Dale's. "I shall see you then."

CHAPTER 3

The following afternoon Mary took the air outside, determined to be outdoors every day no matter the weather. Her mind wandered from thought to thought, or if more truthful, one thought that is. The duke.

Mary wasn't sure what to make of her brother's friend. Of course she'd heard he was a duke well before his arrival at their estate. Peter seemed to get along with him very well, even though the man was a much sought-after gentleman in Town and held a lot of sway within the House of Lords. If her mother's unending information about the duke was to be believed. But there was something about the fellow that gave her pause, a niggling annoyance that she could not place. Something that had troubled her the moment his steely eyes and unflinching inspection of her occurred in the drawing room last evening.

Her friend and companion, Louise, came up beside her as they walked about the grounds; bundled up in fur coats they both appeared three sizes larger than they were. But, when there was snow underfoot and one was stuck indoors, such clothing had to be worn, no matter how bulky. No-one wished to be stuck inside all the time.

"It's so cold, Mary. Can we return indoors now?" Her friend pulled her coat closed further and Mary smiled. Louise had always preferred the warmer months and hated any season other than spring or summer.

"We'll just finish going around the house and then we'll go back inside. It's so refreshing though, don't you think, to be outdoors? With Peter home with his friend, and Mama with her guests, inside is becoming a little crowded."

Louise's eyes glistened with amusement. "What do you think of the duke? I don't think I've ever seen a more handsome fellow in all my life."

"Well, our life has been cosseted here most of the time in Derbyshire. I'm sure when we return to London next year, Town life will offer you more diversion and interest than the Duke of Carlton. It's simply we've been out in the country so long and only ever meet the same people. Anything new and shiny always sparkles brighter."

Her friend snorted. "Are you being sarcastic, dear Mary? I don't think there are many who would not continually be distracted by such a man."

Mary conceded the point. The duke was exceedingly handsome, with his dark locks that had a slight waviness and curl to them. His straight nose and cheekbones made his profile devastatingly lovely and made her stomach flutter each time she chanced a look at him.

Her body was becoming a traitor to her. She didn't want to feel anything other than bored amusement that he was present. Mary certainly didn't want images and thoughts bombarding her mind as to what he might be like to kiss. Was he so very wicked as all the gossips had painted him these past days? There was a rumor that he'd once bedded

Lady Hectorville, and if her ladyship's glances toward the duke when she assumed no one was looking were anything to go by, Mary certainly could believe that tidbit of information as fact.

"Very well, I shall agree with you on that, but even so, he is just a man who'll eventually marry a woman to warm his bed and fill his nursery with heirs for his great title. Whomever the duke marries it'll be a monetary and status alliance, not a love match."

"And to be a power in the *ton*. A duchess that all other women strive to imitate, do not forget," Louise added.

Mary stumbled to a halt. Louise gasped as the duke, whom they'd not seen sitting on the steps of the terrace stood, and bowed before them.

Heat bloomed on Mary's cheeks and her stomach did that stupid little fluttering again. She glared at him. What was wrong with her?

She cleared her throat, clasping her hands tight within her fur muff. "Your grace, we did not see you there."

One ducal eyebrow rose in agreement. "No, you did not. I can only assume that had you known I was sitting here you wouldn't have said such things about my character."

Mary chanced a glance at Louise and sighed at her friend's abject horror of them being caught. If her friend's eyes went any wider her eyeballs would pop out.

She smiled the sweetest smile she could muster for someone who was obviously used to no one talking about him at all. Certainly not to his face. "You would be mistaken, your grace. I never shy away from what I believe in or think. If I have an opinion on a subject or person, whatever it may be, you can always be assured I'll speak the truth."

His too-intelligent eyes inspected her, and Mary shivered. How was it that his mere gaze could make her react so? She fought not to roll her eyes at her own idiocy. Maybe a trip to Town for another Season wasn't such a bad idea after all. This shivering and fluttering whenever she was about the duke would never do. If she had to marry as her parents ordained, then it would be to a man she respected and loved, not to mention a man who allowed her to carry on with all the hobbies she currently enjoyed. She eyed the duke. *What kind of man are you?*

"Perhaps it's the spectacles that make you so forward with your opinion." The duke reached out and slid them off her face. His buckskin-gloved fingers touched her temples and she gasped at his presumption.

"Excuse me, your grace, but just what do you think you're doing?"

She looked up at him, and although she could see perfectly well without glasses, they did help her see objects that were at a distance.

He stared at her for the oddest time before he said, "just seeing what you look like behind your spectacles."

"And do you always do what you want, your grace?" Mary asked, suspecting that he did. The man oozed authority and she doubted there wasn't much that he did not get his way with.

"Always," he said, before turning on his heel and striding toward the terrace doors.

"Well, how odd," Mary said. Louise sighed, a dreamy expression on her face as she watched the duke head back indoors. He closed the terrace doors with a decided click, leaving them alone once again.

Louise caught Mary's gaze. "He still has your spectacles."

After his odd departure Mary had completely forgotten the fact that he'd walked off with her spectacles. She ground her teeth, not wanting to seek him out to get them back again. She huffed out an annoyed breath, supposing she would have to. And after that, it was probably best that she did not seek him out again while he was here. Her body needed to learn that the Duke of Carlton, no matter his attractiveness, was not for her. She had a Season to find a gentleman who would suit her and she would not allow a pretty face to steer her off-course.

*ale shut the terrace doors and leaned against the wooden frame a moment. Feeling something in his hand he looked down and cursed. What the devil was he still doing with Lady Mary's spectacles? And why in hell had he taken them off of her in the first place?

The moment he'd seen her glance up at him, her eyes wide and clear and the prettiest green he'd ever beheld he knew he was in trouble. He didn't need to think her eyes pretty, or anything about her appealing. She was his best friend's sister. A woman who spoke her mind without restraint and obviously was so very used to doing as she pleased. She was certainly not duchess material. Not the type of obedient and placid woman he was looking for.

His mother had been opinionated, often arguing differences of opinion with his father. He didn't want a wife with similar characteristics. He wanted only peace in his marriage, something that he never enjoyed as a child.

Her rebuttal that she would only ever speak the truth whether the person was present or not was proof of that. Even if the *ton* was full of lies and deceit, her frankness was not a character trait he wanted in a wife. There were plenty of gentlemen who did not care if their wives were opinionated. Dale was not one of them.

That she'd not shied away from his sometimes overbearing self, had been welcome however. But then his friend

Peter had never been scared off by his title either, and it was one of the reasons they were friends. He could tell Peter anything and know he would give him the absolute truth in his opinions.

Not just agree with him all the time simply because he was a duke.

Lady Hectorville sidled next to him and placed her arm around his own. He smiled down at her out of politeness while swearing inwardly at her affront. "Lady Hectorville, are you enjoying the gathering here in Derbyshire?" The question was benign, and he hoped soon enough she would find more amusing sports. Her reported lover was present so why she was hanging off his arm was beyond him.

"Oh, indeed I am. Lord and Lady Lancaster have been the most wonderful hosts these past few days and I'm looking very much toward the coming month here, and Christmas of course. Are you staying for the festivities, the Mistletoe Ball, your grace?"

He had thought of staying, but with her ladyship's presence the entire time, maybe Dale would have to rethink his decision. "My obligations are not fixed on any one place in particular. I did say I would stay for a time, but I'm unsure if that will incorporate Christmas."

Lady Hectorville pouted and he turned his attention to the few guests that were taking tea in the parlor. "And your sister, Lady Georgianna? Where is she to spend Christmas this year?"

Dale smiled at the mention of his sibling. He missed the chit and hoped she would be home soon. "She's spending Christmas in Spain with our aunt who's traveling abroad. She'll return to Town in the spring."

"Oh, Spain. How diverting. The warm Spanish sun, the hot nights and even hotter days. Sounds positively divine," she cooed up at him.

He nodded, not entirely sure that the direction in which her ladyship spoke didn't have an altogether different meaning to that of the weather. The terrace doors behind him opened and Lady Mary and her friend, Miss Grant, entered the room. Dale watched their progress as they joined Peter near the pianoforte.

Her ladyship lent out a long-suffering sigh. "Poor Lady Mary, I do worry for her. She's so very bookish and the spectacles she's often sporting do nothing to improve her appearance. I worry that she'll remain a spinster, be placed up on the shelf to collect dust like an unwanted ornament."

Dale bit his tongue in reminding Lady Hectorville that to speak about someone in such a manner was not befitting of her ladyship's status. He thanked a footman for a glass of wine and took a fortifying sip to cool his ire. "Really? Do enlighten me?" he asked, his curiosity to see just how far her ladyship was willing to go further to cast doubt on Mary who was the daughter of a supposedly close friend of hers.

"Well, she does not draw or paint or take any time in needlework from all accounts. Instead she's a dab hand at fishing. Fishing! Of all things and is a better shot than her brother from what Lady Lancaster tells me. The young woman will never make a match with such qualities."

Stranger and stranger. Dale's attention strayed to where Lady Mary stood and he took in her gown, her features and demeanor. She was quite animated and loud, but then she was in her own home and among friends, so one did tend to let their guard down.

Her ebony hair shone as dark as the midnight sky, even when tied up in a severe knot. But with her spectacles missing, one could see the promise of an emerging beauty if one looked hard enough. Her green eyes were certainly one of her best features, and upon meeting her had given a hint to a woman of intelligence.

"I'm sure in time Lady Mary will marry. No matter how society views her as possibly lacking in refinement. There are other qualities that recommend her." Dale shut his mouth with a snap, not knowing why he was defending the woman. Probably because she was Peter's sibling and Peter was his closest friend.

Lady Hectorville clasped her chest. "Oh, I do hope you don't think I meant any slight against Lady Mary. I love her as if she were my own child, but I do like to think that if I were a mother, I too could see the faults in my own children. No matter how disappointing such a thing may be."

"Of course," he said bowing. "If you'll excuse me, Lady Hectorville." He started toward Lady Mary and coming up to Peter, pulled the spectacles from his waistcoat pocket.

"Lady Mary, I do believe these belong to you." He handed them to her and she cast a quick glance at her brother who stood silent, watching them with a warning glint in his eyes.

Dale straightened and clasped his hands behind his back.

"Thank you, your grace."

"What is Carlton doing with your spectacles, Mary?" Peter asked, his tone one of suspicion.

"Lady Mary had been taking the air with Miss Grant and had misplaced the spectacles on the terrace railing. I was merely returning them." Total bollocks, but he didn't need Peter to imagine that there was anything at all between him and his sister for there was not, nor ever would be. She was much too independent, and he had a sneaking suspicion she was a bluestocking as well as a wallflower. His wife would be a demure, quiet type of woman, suited to the role of duchess and all the responsibilities that came with it.

Not to mention he would never jeopardize his friendship with Peter. They had shared many a night out on the town in London, and he doubted Peter would want his sister marrying a man known for his rakish ways.

Peter clasped him on the back, smiling. "Well then, you're a good man. Thank you for giving them back to Mary. She's often doing that, leaving them here and there. Aren't you Mary?" Peter said, turning to her.

"I'm terribly forgetful with those sorts of matters. Thank you, your grace, for returning them to me," she said, before she touched her friend's hand. "Shall we head upstairs, Louise. I wish to read for a time before dinner."

Both ladies left without another word and Peter smiled after them. "What do you think about Miss Grant? She's grown most pretty since I've been away at school. She is Mary's companion and been with us since she was a child."

Dale took another glass of wine from a passing footman thinking over Miss Grant. "Do you care for her? Remember that marriage is a lifelong commitment. I doubt there would be anything worse in the world than to be partnered with a woman who after six months of marriage turned into a shrew and stopped all wifely duties once you'd begotten an heir."

Peter's eyes widened. "Hold up old boy. I only asked what you thought of her. I'm not planning to marry at all at present."

Dale chuckled to break the small tension between them. "You know my thoughts on marriage. It is a decision to be thought over with great care. My parents' match was not a union I would wish upon anyone else, and so I simply do not wish for you to make the same mistake.

The memory of his parents arguing could still, to this day, make his blood run cold. Both were high-handed and never at fault. When both parties refused to give way, let a disagreement go, fireworks were often what resulted. Although Dale never witnessed any physical injury, he had his suspicions that such had taken place behind closed doors.

"Your parents however seem to have a happy and affectionate marriage. Let them guide you and I'm sure they'll do you no wrong."

Peter mumbled something under his breath and Dale thought about what Lady Hectorville had said about staying. Perhaps he ought to return to his own estate before the snow became too thick underfoot for travel. But he did enjoy being with Peter and his family who were jovial and welcoming, even his sister, as odd as she was.

He would think on it some more.

"You missed the announcement at breakfast about our annual Mistletoe Ball; it is to be held again this year. Although really it's just a guise to try and advertise that my sister is still open to marriage and courting if anyone should be interested. Even so, it's always good, jolly fun. What say you?"

"When is this to take place?" Dale asked, not entirely sure he wished to be part of such entertainment. He would have enough of society, all the balls and trappings next year in Town.

"A few days before Christmas. Do say you'll attend. My parents will be sorely disappointed if you leave. Just like myself, we do not wish for you to be alone at Christmas."

That was true, Dale also didn't wish to be alone at such a festive time. Not really. With Georgianna away in Spain, Carlton Hall was large and very empty, almost like a crypt. Not a place to enjoy the holiday season when alone.

"Very well, I shall stay until after Christmas as planned. I suppose I shall be able to stomach a ball well enough."

"Excellent," Peter said. "Now come, let's go play some billiards. I think we've done the pretty by my mother and given the guests here today enough fodder to keep them happy for an afternoon or so."

Dale liked the thought of that. "Lead the way." Escaping the afternoon at home sounded right up his alley.

Just then the door to the parlor opened and in walked Henry Ryley, Lord Weston. New to the title of Viscount, the young buck had made a debutante cry during her first ball. He was as obnoxious as he was stupid. Dale sighed, wondering why in the hell Lord Lancaster had invited such a dandy.

The viscount strolled into the room, greeting his hosts and looking about as if he owned the place. He was all blond, his golden locks and height made him most agreeable to the ladies present if their tittering and simpering smiles were anything to go by.

Dale looked about the room and fought not to roll his eyes as some of the younger women giggled and blushed.

"Weston," Peter yelled out, catching the young man's attention. He strolled over.

"Kensley," his lordship said, shaking Peter's hand. "It's good to see you. How have you been? I've not seen you in Town of late."

"No," Peter said, smiling. "I've been traveling in the country for some weeks." Peter turned to Dale. "Your grace, this is Viscount Weston. Lord Weston, this is his grace, the Duke of Carlton."

Dale bowed slightly.

"Pleasure, your grace. In fact, I've just come from the stables and been admiring your gray stallion. Beautiful beast if ever there was one," Lord Weston said jovially.

Dale narrowed his eyes. "He's a good horse," was all he was able to manage while also trying to remember what debutante it was that this popinjay insulted and what that insult had been about.

"Is Mary home? I should like to see her again. I've been so busy in Town this past Season that I did not get to see her much."

Peter smiled at the mention of his sister. Dale arched a

brow. Lord Weston was on a first-name basis with Lady Mary? He studied the man with a disinterested air. As little as he knew Lady Mary, it would be a shame indeed if she set her cap for someone like Lord Weston.

"She's gone upstairs to read before dinner, but you'll see her later. She'll be so excited to see you again too. I know how close you were as children."

"You've known the family for some time then, Lord Weston?" Dale asked, curiosity getting the better of him.

The young viscount glanced at Dale with annoyance and there was something in his gaze that gave Dale pause. If he were a betting man, he would lay money on the fact that his lordship had a nasty streak in his blood. He'd seen glances like the one his lordship just bestowed on him, his father had thrown them often toward his mother before all hell broke loose. Here, Dale supposed he could not cause any mischief, even if the question had annoyed the gentleman.

"Lord Weston and our family are neighbors, your grace," Peter said, answering the question quickly.

He took a sip of his wine, glad to hear this was how they were acquainted, not by some other means such as Weston's courtship of Lady Mary. "Are you staying or merely visiting, Lord Weston?" Dale asked. Normally a good judge of character, there was something about this man that he didn't like. Finally, the memory came back to him as to why he disapproved of the viscount. The young debutante he'd made cry had been courted by his lordship for weeks, so much so that the family had expected an offer of marriage. Instead, he'd ceased all contact with the chit and refused to stand up with her at balls and parties. She became the target of censure and amusement for her friends. The young woman had returned to the country and Dale wondered if she would return next year and try again. Something told him she would not.

"I'm staying," the gentleman said, raising his brow and holding Dale's gaze.

Dale narrowed his eyes. "I see."

The young viscount spied another guest he wished to speak to, and he made his farewells.

"Shall we?" Peter said, gesturing toward the door.

Dale nodded. "Yes, let's go."

CHAPTER 4

*M*ary came downstairs later that evening and found Lord Weston present. She had not expected him to arrive since when she had seen him last Season in Town he'd been less than pleased to greet her. His slight, even if not noticed by the *ton* had hurt more than she'd been willing to admit even to her parents and she had eventually talked herself into believing that it was all in her mind.

And so it seemed to be if his animation and pleasure at seeing her again was anything to go by.

"Lord Weston. Henry," she said, using his given name, "it is so very good to see you." She came up to him and laughed when he pulled her into an embrace. Her parents smiled at their familiarity, and didn't seem inclined to chastise her over their conduct.

"It is good to see you again too, Mary and Miss Grant as well. I'm sorry I'm late to arrive. I've only just returned from London."

Mary smiled at his lordship who seemed very happy indeed to be back in Derbyshire and talking to her. For years she'd harbored a little infatuation for his lordship. How could one not be with his golden locks and sinful gaze that made him look like a fallen angel? Mary might be somewhat skewed against marriage, but she was not blind.

She supposed she had gravitated toward him so often because she'd known him since childhood and deep down knew he'd never look to her as a wife, and so he was a safe option to be amusing with.

"Well, you're here now and that's all that matters. Mama has invited quite a few families from Town so you should feel quite at home."

"I'm sure I shall," he said, smiling down at her.

Mary's stomach flipped a little and she had to force herself to glance away from all his grandeur. How handsome he was. His perfect nose and lovely clear blue eyes that set him apart from most men.

Mary's gaze slid to the Duke of Carlton's, surprised to find his eyes narrowed in contemplation as he watched them. She turned her attention back to Lord Weston. The duke was too good-looking for his own good as well, and probably well aware of it.

The dinner gong sounded and forgoing formalities, her parents led everyone into the dining room. The dinner was five courses of fish and game, turtle soup and winter vegetables. No expense was spared for their guests and Mary would commend their cook on her dinner later that evening. The dinner lasted some hours, all of them enjoyable, full of conversation and laughter. Just as this festive time of year ought to be.

Mistletoe ran along the center of the table with cuttings of holly to add a little color to the decoration. With the fires burning in every room, their mammoth home was transformed into a wonderland of Yuletide and cheer.

After dinner Mary sat near the edge of the drawing room, watching those in attendance. She sipped her mulled wine and listened while Louise played a Christmas tune on the pianoforte.

Her stomach fluttered as Lord Weston made his way toward her, his smile as wicked as ever. She'd known him most of her life, and there was something about him that she'd always been drawn to. Perhaps it was the fact he was in reality unattainable. She was no elegant, ethereal-looking beauty, she was dark of hair, and eyes a plain, unremarkable green. Her skin looked kissed by the sun.

And he was simply too perfect to ever look at her. They were as opposite as night and day.

"All alone, Mary? We're missing your company and so I've come to drag you back into the fray."

She smiled, inwardly sighing at his beauty. For a moment her gaze slid to his lips, pulled back to show perfectly straight white teeth. He had lovely lips too. In all honesty there wasn't much about him that wasn't faultless.

"A moment's peace I assure you, but I shall mingle in a little while. We have missed you these past months. Have you enjoyed Town this Season?"

He leaned back in his chair, sliding his arm to sit along the back of her own and she started when his thumb reached out and circled the bare skin on her shoulder. "I did, but I would prefer a stroll outdoors with you in its stead? I know it's cold, but I remember that such a thing never bothered you before."

Mary jumped up, not sure her heart could take any more of his touch. "I'm not sure that is wise…"

His lordship stood, mischief in his gaze. "Come, it's only a stroll. We're old friends, and have walked outdoors numerous times. No harm will come to you, I promise."

Mary glanced at her mother and seeing her nod of approval, relented. "Very well, my lord. Let me grab my shawl."

Only minutes later they made their way out onto the terrace which had earlier today been shoveled free of snow. A light dusting covered the flagstones still, and the chill was beyond what she expected. Their outing would be of short duration.

The glow from the windows lit their way as they strolled slowly along. Mary glanced out into the gardens, not sure what Lord Weston wanted to discuss with her, if anything.

"We have always been friends, have we not, Mary?"

He said, pulling her to a stop. Her elbow burned from his touch and her heart thumped loud in her chest. More so than it ever had before.

"Of course. Why do you ask?" She glanced up at him, a tentative smile on her lips. Was Lord Weston looking to court her? Mary thought over the possibility a moment. He would certainly suit her character and most importantly he was their neighbor here in Derbyshire. She would not have to leave the lands that she'd grown up on. She could remain close to her parents and her brother when he decided to marry.

She'd not thought of the viscount as an option before, but all night he'd made certain to remain close to her. His lordship knew of her love for the outdoors, for fishing and hunting and was only ever supportive of it. He would not try and change her ways, or make her conform to society…

His attention snapped to her lips and all thought flew out of her brain.

"Have you ev–"

Mary lunged at his head, kissing him before he could finish what he was about to say. Their teeth cracked together and horrified Mary felt blood across her tongue as she slid back to earth. She stepped back, heat suffusing her body at the bumbling fool she'd just been.

"I'm sorry, my lord. I do not know…"

He stared at her, his visage one of shock and pity and if the earth could swallow her she hoped it would do so right at this moment.

He cleared his throat, pulling out his handkerchief and dabbing at his lip that horrifyingly was bleeding. "I think you should return indoors, Mary. I need to ice my lip and will return to the drawing room soon."

She nodded, feeling all kinds of stupid. No refined gentleman such as Lord Weston would look at her with anything other than sympathy and she was a fool to think he harbored ideas of them marrying.

Mary glanced down at her gown of lace and ribbons, absurd bows that were not the least fashionable on anyone over the age of five. "I apologize, Lord Weston. It will not happen again."

She ran, heedless of everything about her, and instead of returning to the drawing room, she entered another door further along that opened into a corridor toward the conservatory.

Mary stifled back a sob as the prickling of tears stung her eyes. Her past five Seasons had been all disasters, and now, after trying to kiss one of her oldest friends she would prefer to die of mortification than have to face him again.

She rounded a corner that led into the conservatory and clashed straight into a wall of muscle. Strong arms came out about her, but her near run had too much momentum and she took him down, landing with a thump on top of him.

"Oh, I'm terribly sorry."

Mary went to roll off him and heard a rip near her breast. Looking down she spied one of the gentleman's buttons on his superfine coat was hooked onto one of her lace ribbons.

"I'm stuck," she mumbled, placing her legs on either side of him so to free her hands and try and unhook herself from the gentleman. His own hands came around her and he sat up, bringing her with him. She gasped, forgetting the button and ribbon as she glanced up and died a second time that night of mortification.

"Your grace, I did not know…that is to say," she fumbled for words. "I do apologize for this."

He stared at her with dark hooded eyes, his mouth set in a thin displeased line. He was angry at her. She expected no less after tackling him just now.

"Here let me." His fingers joined with hers as they both fumbled to remove the button from the lace. Their heads bent close Mary caught a whiff of his scent, sandalwood and something else, something sweet and delicious that made one want cake.

The duke mumbled something unintelligible, and unable to help herself she looked at him instead of concentrating on trying to remove herself from his lap. Up close he was as handsome as any she'd seen, even Lord Weston who was pretty where the duke was like a replica of a chiseled god.

Certainly the duke's shoulders were wider than Lord Weston's, and his legs seemed quite muscular between her own. The thought brought awareness as to how they were sitting. She on top of his lap, her skirts hiked up about her waist and a…what was that hard bulge near her inner thigh?

She gasped and their gazes locked. Mumbling a curse, one she heard as clear as day, the duke ripped them apart, the lace ribbon now an ornament upon his own button before he picked her up and deposited her on the floor beside him.

He stood, his back to her as he adjusted his clothing. Mary could do little but stare at his back, the view from down on the floor giving her the perfect location to study the duke's other assets, like his bottom.

His Grace turned, the muscle in his jaw flexing when he caught her ogling his person. Instead of turning from her in disgust, he reached out a hand to help her up. "In a rush, Lady Mary?"

All thoughts of Lord Weston fled from her mind after being entwined with the duke, and she gaped at him a moment trying to remember what her flight into the conservatory was about.

And then she remembered. Her first kiss. Or, perhaps she ought to remember it by the first bloody lip she'd given a gentleman with her own mouth.

"I apologize again, your grace. I needed to be alone and didn't expect to find anyone in this part of the house."

He studied her, his brow furrowed. "Is something amiss? You look as if you've been crying."

She swallowed, shame washing over her in spades. Mary looked down at her feet, working her hands before her. "I made a mistake that I cannot take back and now I'll never be able to face a certain person ever again." Very well, it may have been a little over-dramatic, but the thought of what she'd done, of how Lord Weston had reacted, it certainly felt as though her life would never be the same. If only she'd not tried to kiss him. What had she been thinking!

His warm hand clasped her elbow and he led her into the conservatory. "Come and sit. I know we do not know each other well, and maybe that will make it easier to unburden yourself."

She sat on the cold marble seat and went to pull her shawl about her arms, only to find it missing. She looked back out into the hall where she had collided with the duke and spied it on the floor.

"Are you sure you wish to hear about my antics, your grace?" she said, huddling a little into herself, the room chilly in the night air. The duke shuffled off his coat and slipped it about her shoulders. His heat engulfed her, settling about her a notion of calm.

"Of course I'll listen to you. Whatever you have to say."

Mary bit her lip, reminded of what had happened with Lord Weston. The words spilled from her over what she'd done and how his lordship had reacted. Why she was telling his grace this information she did not know or understand, but his offering to hear her concerns were kindly meant and he was Peter's friend after all. Peter would never be close with anyone if they did not have his trust. And heaven helped her, she desperately wanted to tell someone about what happened. "Lord Weston looked at me as if I'd grown two heads," she continued. "I know I'm not as fashionable as other women in Town." She gestured to her dress and the duke looked her over, pity entering his gray orbs. "I'm opinionated and perhaps a little wild. I ran into you and entangled myself in your buttons. But my parents are adamant I marry, and I worry that I'll make the wrong choice. I do not wish to be trapped in an unhappy union." She looked up at him and held his gaze. "Please tell me not all gentlemen are looking for simpering debutantes with no voice."

*D*ale stared at Lady Mary, utterly enthralled by her zest to make men see women, women such as herself more than the fripperies their mamas dressed them up in. To admire women who were educated and opinionated. Dale could admit that he might be a little biased against such features. He could only assume because his mother had been such a woman, and it had always brought out the worst in his father.

Dale sighed, patting her hand in comfort. "Unfortunately, Lady Mary, men are not always that bright of mind." *He certainly was not.* "Having a sister of my own, I've come to realize that the female sex is more often than not more calm and thoughtful toward others. Of course you get some degree to all sexes that are not so, and you're not different."

She threw him a cautious smile and he noticed her dark, long eyelashes. Not to mention in the scuffle in the hall, her hair had come loose of some of the pins and cascaded over her delicate shoulders. His gaze shifted lower at he drank in the bountiful breasts that sat hidden beneath the ribbons and lace.

That he knew what she felt like in his arms also did not help his constitution.

"How will I ever face him again? I'm mortified."

Dale placed his arm about her shoulders, rubbing her arm in comfort. "You will face him like you would anyone. You will raise your chin and think no more of it. We've all made mistakes such as the one you made today. Laugh it off and forget about it. It was only a kiss after all."

He looked over to a potted rose across from them, but all he could smell was Lady Mary and the sweet scent of jasmine.

"He's so very well received in Town. He'll never speak to me again, he'll probably laugh at me and call me a silly child who needs to grow up."

"Are you?" Dale asked, meeting her gaze when she glanced at him.

"Am I what?" she asked, her eyes bright with unshed tears.

"A silly chit who needs to grow up?"

She pulled back a little, clearly affronted. "Of course not!"

He shrugged. "Well then, you have nothing to worry about."

She sighed, her breasts rising at the action. He tore his gaze away, concentrating on the plants about him. "I don't know how to be fashionable and worldly. I'm simply too rough about the edges to ever change, I believe. I don't particularly want a husband, but if I do have to marry, Lord

Weston does suit my requirements. He's our neighbor and we've known him for years, so he knows me very well. Knows that I'm too set in my ways now to change. You see, your grace," she said, sitting back. "I like to experience all things. To be well versed in life. We must read, love, laugh and play. Swim, fish, dance and…"

Dale removed his arm and watched her patiently. "Kiss," he ventured, inexplicably entranced by her. He watched her, the line of her neck as she glanced up at the glass roof, looking at the stars beyond.

"And kiss," she whispered, longing echoing in her voice.

Her eyes met his and a heady, dark emotion swirled inside Dale. This girl, woman, he should amend was dangerous to men like him. Such little temptresses made them want things they would otherwise steer clear of.

He sighed, studying her a moment. As much as he disliked Lord Weston, if that was whom Lady Mary thought would suit her temperament and character, who was he to naysay her? "I'll tell you what, Lady Mary. Do you want me to help you regain your Lord Weston and have him eating out of your hand like a puppy for the remainder of this house party?"

Her eyes brightened, making her more beautiful than he thought possible. Damn it all to hell he didn't need to think of her in such a way. He cleared his throat. "I will give you one piece of advice, and you must follow it. To the letter." Dale paused, looking down his nose at her. "Are we in agreement."

"Oh yes." She nodded eagerly, which jiggled her breasts in his peripheral vision. *Dear Lord in heaven he was in hell.*

"I would suggest you be honest with Lord Weston. If you think he suits you, then let him know that you're open to courtship. Be flirty, charming, and honest with him. Forget about the kiss, his reaction, all of it. Lift that pretty face of yours and look him in the eyes, be bold and forthright. Talk of more than the weather, discuss what you enjoy, what you love to do, and if he is not a fool, he will fall at your feet. I promise you that."

"Is that what you like, your grace?" she asked.

Dale started at her question before he stood, needing to distance himself. "I respect honesty above everything else."

"Thank you, your grace," she said, standing. "My brother normally has good sense and I see he had the good sense to befriend you. You're an honorable man." She held out her gloved hand and he reached for it, bringing it to his lips and bowing over it slightly.

"Good luck, Lady Mary and may the man who deserves you win."

She threw him a dazzling smile, striding to where they had clashed, swooping up her shawl, she glanced back at him one last time before she was gone. He smiled after her, shaking his head in amusement. This country retreat had just become more interesting. Now he could sit back and watch the games unfold. Or at least, the one Lady Mary was playing.

CHAPTER 5

*M*ary spent the following day adjusting all her gowns. She would not wait until next Season as discussed with her father, she would alter the dresses she wore now to suit her better. Mary tore at lace and ribbons, lowered her necklines and removed any sort of frippery that decorated her dresses. Underneath all the accessories, her dresses were handsome enough and would do before she could order a new wardrobe next Season.

Mary assessed her handiwork, unable to fathom why she'd allowed the hideous adornments for so long.

Tonight she would put into place the recommendation the Duke of Carlton had suggested to her. She would be feminine but intelligent with conversations that were worthy of discussion amongst the opposite sex. She would laugh in a sultry manner, but remain ladylike, show interest in the opposite sex, instead of indifference like she'd always done before. That, along with her own modifications, namely her clothing and hair would give her an idea of how she would go when back in London. Mary had also gone as far as to ask her mother's lady's maid to style her hair in a more modern style, some tendrils falling softly about her face and making her look more worldly than a country lady. All that was left for her to do was dress.

There was a quick knock on the door before her friend Louise bustled into the room. Louise was already dressed for dinner and she looked lovely as usual with her petite frame and pretty smile.

Louise stopped inside the door, shutting it behind her. "Oh, Mary, your hair looks marvelous. So much more elegant and suitable for your age."

Her maid blushed, clearly pleased with herself and Mary smiled. "I cannot thank you both enough for helping me today with everything that I asked. I should have acted before now regarding my gowns instead of thinking of mother's feelings. I wasn't actively seeking a husband before though, and so didn't see the point. But if I am to marry as my father has stated, I need to be more amenable and willing to talk to gentlemen, open and honestly. If I am more willing, maybe I will find someone who will suit my character better." The more Mary thought about this, the more it made sense to her. Instead of dismissing, but engaging, she might find a gentleman who would allow her pursuits to continue and the marriage would be a happy one for both involved.

Louise nodded. "It is certainly worth a try. There are marriages made within the *ton* which are grand love matches all the time. There is no reason why yours will not be."

"Like who?" Mary asked, lifting her arms so her maid could help her into her gown.

Louise blinked, biting her lip. "Well…I cannot remember at the moment, but I'm sure there are such couples."

Mary stifled a laugh. "In any case, we had better finish getting dressed for dinner, there is still much to be done."

After much cutting and re-stitching, the dress Mary wore tonight was the most revealing she'd ever worn. The sapphire silk set off her dark hair and sun-kissed skin. There were no bows or ribbons, no gaudy lace or high necklines, this gown was simple yet fashionable. Simply perfect for her first night in proving that although she might like the outdoors, fishing, and shooting, swimming in the summer, that did not mean she could not also be a lady.

She stood before the cheval mirror, taking in her appearance. To finish off her ensemble her maid placed a small sapphire that hung from a delicate gold chain about her neck. The final piece of her transformation. Mary smiled, not recognizing the woman staring back at her. She looked completely different and yet the girl gazing back was also the same. And she liked what she saw.

"You look beautiful," Louise said, coming up behind her and catching her eye in the mirror.

Nerves fluttered in Mary's stomach and nodded, raising her chin, ready to face her future. "I think this will do well enough."

*D*ale stood conversing with Lady Hectorville who had cornered him the moment he came downstairs. Her whispered words and sultry tone had worked on him once, on a night he had been in his cups and not himself. Her seduction that evening had worked, but not this night. Not ever again.

Why her ladyship continued to seek him out for bed sport baffled him, and in truth had started to become a nuisance.

Did she not have better things to do with her time? The woman really needed a hobby. If she didn't find something other than men to occupy her time, she'd soon end up with syphilis.

The door to the front reception room where everyone was gathered before dinner opened, and Dale glanced toward the new arrivals. Taking a sip of his whisky, he coughed, choking on his drink at the sight of Lady Mary. Lady Hectorville glanced at him sharply and he cleared his throat, schooling his features into a mask of indifference.

But boredom was the least of his emotions at that moment. Like a moth to a flame, so too was Dale's attention riveted on her. Lady Mary greeted her mama, curtsying and smiling as her mother gushed over her daughter's stunning appearance. Minus the lace and bows that normally adorned her gowns, but something else was different too. Her hair had been styled to better suit her age, and gave one the opportunity to admire her lovely neck.

"She is very beautiful tonight. I did say to Lady Lancaster that she should allow Mary to wear clothes that were more fashionable and popular among the young set, but my friend is so set in her ways. But la, look at Mary now. A woman, not a young girl in braids anymore," Lady Hectorville said.

That was certainly true. The bountiful décolletage was proof of that. And she was only five years younger than himself, not an old maid at all. If she were to attend London next year wearing such gowns she would find a husband soon enough.

The thought left him cold and he took a sip of his whisky, tearing his regard from the delectable little morsel. A hot, and urgent need sat heavy in his gut and he took a few calming breaths. *Remember she is not for you.* And while he knew it, Dale still allowed his gaze to return to her and to bask in the idea, just for a moment, what it would be like to kiss her...and perhaps have her lips curve in that pretty smile just for him. To date he'd yet to find a lady who made him want to give up his more sensual pursuits and settle into domesticity. But the desire coursing through his veins now made him really look at Lady Mary. Dale frowned. She was fire...and fire with fire was never a good combination. No... for whenever he decided to take the plunge into matrimony, it must be a lady of cool demureness. With admirable willpower he tore his stare from her.

☙

*H*uffing out a disgruntled breath, Lady Hectorville flounced off. He glanced to his side as the sweet scent of roses caught his attention and his lips twitched into a grin. "Good evening, Lady Mary. You look very fetching tonight, although I think you're already aware of that."

She grinned mischievously, taking a glass of wine from a footman who bowed before her. "I am being more practical in my choosing of a husband and will take heed of your advice and be more personable, more interested, but I also needed to make a few changes myself." She glanced down at her gown and drew his attention there also. "I shall have Mama purchase a new wardrobe next year, but the alterations to my gowns I have made today will do well enough until then."

His gaze moved over her, taking in the narrowing of her waist beneath the silk dress. She was very fetching in it. The empire cut suited her body shape, and Dale couldn't help but wonder if her hips were as bountiful as her breasts.

Dale took another sip of his whisky and mortifyingly found it empty. She chuckled and he knew she'd seen his lapse in concentration.

"Let me get you another." She waved a footman over.

"Thank you," he said, heat flaming his cheeks. He cleared his throat. "So, you're going to take heed of some of my recommendations. I do hope you find them beneficial."

She bit her lip and he ground his teeth. A woman who

was utterly clueless that she was charming was nothing short of dangerous. "Well, I think what you said made sense. If I can hold an intelligent conversation with a man perhaps I'll like him enough to allow him to court me. As much as I'd love to keep escaping the marriage trap, I know I cannot do so forever," she whispered, leaning close to him and giving him a good view of her bust and the white chemise that sat against her skin.

Damn she was the sweetest thing he wanted to taste, savor and enjoy every ounce of her.

"Lord Weston has not brought up my lapse in conduct since it occurred. I'm glad we've been able to get along just as we ever have."

Dale narrowed his eyes at her tone that although determined, did hold an edge of longing to it. "Is Lord Weston a gentleman whom you would consider a possible suitor?" Dale turned and watched the viscount, dismissing him as a scoundrel and a vain one at that. Certainly not worthy of a free spirit like the intelligent Lady Mary.

She lifted her face and gave him her profile as she glanced across the room to where Lord Weston stood talking to Lady Hectorville. Her ladyship all but hanging off the young lord's every word. His lordship eating up the attention like a glutton.

"Father and mama would certainly approve, and as I said, he's our neighbor. I would not have to move out of the county and I would be close to home. But I promise I will not rush into anything that I'm not certain of. After five Seasons in Town, you must believe that of me, if nothing else."

A light blush rose on her cheeks at the mention of it and he wanted to reach out and see if her skin was as heated as it looked. "Are you ashamed?"

One delicate shoulder lifted in a shrug. Dale tore his gaze away from her person. In all seriousness, did she have to keep reminding him of what lay beneath her gown? It was bad enough that he knew he could never have her. Not in the way he'd like to.

The idea of her beneath him, her hair mussed from bed sport, her lips swollen and red from his kisses, her body marked from where he'd dragged his lips from the tops of her nipples to the core of herself. She'd never think of the washed out popinjay Lord Weston again if he did act on his desires.

A clap on his shoulder startled him and his whisky spilled over his coat sleeve.

Peter laughed. "Ho there, my friend. I did not mean to startle you so."

Dale placed the tumbler aside, pulling out his handkerchief to dab at his jacket. "I did not see you come over, that is all."

"Brother," Lady Mary said, looking less than pleased that her sibling had decided to join them.

"Mary," Peter said in return in just as bored a tone. "Should you not be talking to the eligible gentlemen here instead of boring my friend with your nonsense? To mingle will be good practice for next Season."

She sighed, rolling her eyes. "Charming. And I should hope I wasn't boring you, your grace. I think I can say with honesty that we're friends and can speak plainly."

Dale caught Peter's eye and didn't miss the flicker of contemplation in his friend's orbs. "Of course we're friends, Lady Mary." When he didn't venture to say anything further, she made her excuses and left to sit beside her friend on a nearby settee.

"I do apologize, Carlton. My sister is a little eccentric and straightforward to the point of being blunt. If she's said anything inappropriate, I shall speak to her about it."

Dale shook his head, dismissing the idea. He actually

liked the fact that Lady Mary spoke her mind. The *ton* was full of lies and intrigues and quite rightly, he never enjoyed that side of society.

"She did not bother me."

"Huh," his friend said. "Well, let me know if she does. Even if you are a duke and a good prospect for many beautiful women, my sister is not one of them. She needs to understand that."

Dale frowned, not for the first time feeling as though Peter thought him unworthy of his sister. "Why would you say that? Am I not suitable for your sister?" The question was asked before he could rip it back. What was he saying?

Peter's eyes widened. "Oh, you're a good enough catch and suitable for her of course, but we're friends and she's my sister. Do not forget I know how much of a rogue you are, and have shared in your wild nights in London. She would not do for you."

Something about Peter's tone put him on edge and he bit back an impertinent retort. Instead, he said, "From what you stated yourself we would make a good match, so do explain why we would not." Dale knew what he was saying. It was because of his antics in Town, how he lived. The hard way in which he existed. Nights out at gambling dens, endless balls and parties, women who fell at his feet willing to warm his bed. That Peter knew and had partaken in his lifestyle was reason enough his friend would push his sister away from his orbit, even so, it rankled.

"Mary will marry for love or not at all. If there is one thing that I know about my sister it is that," Peter said, smiling a little to try and dispel the tension that had risen between them.

Dale stared at his friend, hating the fact that Peter thought so little of him. "And she could not love me?"

Peter glanced at him, wide-eyed. "Could you love her

enough to change your ways? To stop your nights of debauchery, of gambling, of flirting with every beautiful woman who crosses your path? You my friend are a wild one, and I daresay only a very biddable wife would condone your rakehell ways. That woman is not my sister and the sparks that would fly would be quite terrifying."

Dale turned his attention back to the gathered guests, not sure he could answer such a question at this time. He would be a good catch for any eligible woman, even Peter's sister, but he would not pursue her. Not because it was obvious Peter did not think he was suited to her, or her needs, but because Dale didn't want to marry just yet. A marriage, to him, was something toxic, a partnership that put people at odds and made them do emotionally damaging things to one another. If he ever married, his wife would be a quiet, biddable woman. She would know her role as duchess better than anything else, and therefore they would never come to odds. Lady Mary was not that woman. To imagine a life with Mary made him envision confrontations, arguments and debates. His gut churned at the memory of his parents' disagreements.

"I could not," he said, agreeing with Peter. "I hope the next Season has a happier ending for Lady Mary than the last."

At that moment the dinner gong sounded somewhere in the depth of the home, and they made their way into the dining room. The night passed well enough, but being seated across from Lady Mary, Dale couldn't help but listen to her conversation with Lord Fairchild, an eligible Marquess from Kent. They spoke of geography and touched on the geology of certain areas about England. The types of fish that his lordship's lakes boasted and that his lordship would enjoy a spot of ice fishing while at Bran Manor. Her carefree laugh, free from restraint or what was expected of a woman of her rank made him smile. Somehow Lady Mary made him yearn for a life he'd never thought to have. Of a marriage where intelligent conversation was to be had, not just about gossip or gowns, or who had a new paramour, but real things. Things that impacted their life, like politics, family, wants and needs. It seemed Lord Fairchild was also thinking the same.

Dale glared at the fellow, tearing his gaze away to look further along the table. He caught Peter's regard, the hardened line of his jaw letting Dale know he'd caught him watching his sister.

He turned back to his meal and Miss Grant, his dinner companion seated to his left, determined to put out of his mind Lady Mary. If not for her sake, then at least for the sake of his friendship with Peter.

CHAPTER 6

*S*ince her transformation Mary had started to enjoy the country house party, and even didn't mind the fact that she could not go outdoors as much as she'd like. Lord Weston plus a flurry of other young gentlemen had been most attentive since she'd updated her gowns to be more fashionable. Allowed herself to be more open to the concept of courtship and Mary found not all of the men were unlikable. Lord Fairchild loved his country estate and spent many months there instead of in Town.

Perhaps finding a husband who suited her was not such an impossibility as she'd thought.

This morning however she would leave the guests and go for a well-deserved ride, having sent word to the stables earlier to have her mare Pegasus saddled. The air was crisp, cutting even, as she started toward the stables, but with her bottle-green riding habit, leather kid gloves, fur cap and scarf, her short ride would not be too taxing. And she needed to get outdoors, to feel the air on her face, be alone to think and relax and not have to be the person that society wished her to be. A woman who stitched before the fire and played piano instead of going outdoors in inclement weather. A woman who was demure and without opinions of her own, everything that she was not.

She started over the northern hill at the back of the property taking Pegasus at a slower pace than usual. With the snow underfoot, not too thick to stop all riding thankfully, but even so, it was thick enough to miss something in the undergrowth, to cause her horse to misstep and possibly hurt itself.

This side of the property was left to grow as nature intended and with very little maintenance from their gardening staff. It made for better hunting seasons and always ensured the sport was good when the gentlemen came up for shooting parties. Mary made her way to the shooting lodge, a sanctuary for herself when not in use. That the lodge also had a stable, always well kept no matter what the time of year, which meant she could place Pegasus in a stall and wile away the day reading, strolling the nearby woods, or simply enjoying her own company.

She rode Pegasus up to the stable door and frowned when she spied it slightly ajar. Had she left it open when she'd been here last? That was a month or so ago, or had one of the groundskeepers accidentally forgotten to lock up when checking on the place. Mary slid off looking about to see if she could see anyone else about.

She walked up to the door and peering inside saw a horse munching hay in one of the stalls, the saddle laying over the stall door and bridle too. Relief ran through her followed by confusion. Whose horse was that?

She turned about, searching, but couldn't see anyone. Was the intruder inside the lodge? Was he living there without the family knowing? Not letting Pegasus go, she walked over to the lodge and peered through a window, her stomach turning into knots as she recognized the man lazing away on a settee beside a window. Without a care in the world, his boots sat up on the chair arm, his arm casually resting behind his head while the other held a book.

In this relaxed stance the Duke of Carlton looked even more devastatingly handsome than he did in a ballroom. Or across the dinner table watching her all night.

Mary turned back to the stable and settled Pegasus before entering the lodge without knocking. This was her lodge after all, or at least her family's and she had more right than the duke to be here. The thought boosted her courage that he might be annoyed at being interrupted.

He started, dropped his book on his lap, and partly sat up when she entered. Realizing it was only her, he chuckled in evident pleasure, and her treasonous body fluttered at the sight of him.

"You scared me, Lady Mary. I did not think anyone would find me hidden away out here at this time of year."

Mary pulled off her fur cap and laid it on a nearby table. She went to stand beside the fire, which was burning fiercely and warming the room. "You have found my sanctuary, your grace. I often come out here to do exactly as you're doing. Today I needed a little peace, the guests have been locked away inside for some days now, and I think some are getting a little sick of the indoors." And she was getting sick of some of them.

He cocked his eyebrow. "You more than most, I assume?"

She nodded once. "You assume correctly, but," she said, gesturing to his book, "I'm more than willing to leave you in peace and come back tomorrow. I do not want to intrude." Even though this was her hunting lodge, the duke was here first and she was unchaperoned.

He sat up, placing the book beside him. The action brought home once again how broad he was across the shoulders, his muscular thighs and large hands. The memory

51

of him holding her after she'd run into him floated through her mind, bringing with it other thoughts. Of his hands running over her body, pulling her close, teasing her every nerve and making her shiver.

"Please, stay. You're shivering and obviously cold. Let me fetch some water and we shall make some tea."

Mary didn't correct his assumption about her shivers. She glanced down, pulling off her gloves, controlling herself not to gawk at him as he stood. He collected the old metal kettle from a nearby bench and started for the door. As much as she tried, her gaze sought him out through her lashes and she admired the view of him from behind as he went out the door.

Upon being left alone, she sighed. Whoever married the duke would be a very lucky woman. The idea of being ravished by him was almost enough to drive all thoughts of anyone else out of her head. Certainly Lord Weston didn't bring forth the ideas and imaginings that the duke did. Nor Lord Fairchild for that matter.

She contemplated that point before he returned and placed the water on the little grill that sat over the flames. He returned to his chair, and folding his legs he asked, "What else do you like to do, Lady Mary, other than sneaking away to hunting lodges when no one is looking?"

His lazy smile made her blood warm. Mary sat, pulling her legs up under her and clasping a nearby pillow to lean against. "Do you really wish to know, your grace?" Not many gentlemen ever cared to know how women passed their time, but then nothing the duke had done since she'd met him had actually made any sense and so she was willing to give him the benefit of her doubts if he really wished to know.

He threw her a half smile. "I would not have asked if I were not interested."

The duke was becoming more interesting by the minute. "I'm especially fond of fishing both in the winter and summer months. I love to swim and I've been practicing rock climbing of late. As you know we have some very good peaks here in Derbyshire."

A small furrow appeared between his brows. "You like to climb rocky outcrops? Is that not dangerous? Do your parents know you take part in such a sport?"

He looked at her as if she'd lost half her mind.

Mary shrugged. "Do not tell my parents, they do not know. And I have taken precautions and secured some ropes. It's all perfectly safe, so long as they hold."

He contemplated her for a long moment, and she fought not to fidget in her chair. How was he able to make her feel all warm and fuzzy every time she was around him? He made her want other things so very different to how her life was at present. Her own home, a marriage, children, all things she'd not had longed for before. She frowned, the thought was as perplexing as it was frightening.

"You should not be climbing rocks by yourself, Lady Mary. What if you fell? It could be days, weeks even, before anyone found you in these parts. You could be long expired by then."

All true, and nothing she'd not thought about herself, but all her hobbies were an escape of duty and she would be loath to have to stop. It was who she was after all, to pretend to be anyone else was impossible to imagine.

"I never climb overly high, but I like the thrill of it." She sighed, smiling at the thought that next year would be her last opportunity to be so carefree. Unless she found a husband who allowed her to continue her passions. "It's such a rush when I reach the peak, makes me simply want to do it again and again."

The duke shifted in his chair and cleared his throat. "Tea, I think."

✦

*D*ale didn't move from his chair. He knew he ought to get up and help Lady Mary with the teacups, sugar and teapot, but he simply could not move. Not yet at least. After her little chat about rock climbing, reaching peaks and wanting to do it again and again, all he could think about was what she would look like beneath him, giving and gaining pleasure.

The hardness in his pants would be obvious to even a blind person, and so he sat, trying to imagine anything other than the little minx before him, writhing, gasping, biting that sweet bottom lip of hers as he brought them both to climax.

He groaned, flopping his head back to look up at the ceiling. He was a veritable ass. A blaggard who could think of nothing but plucking this sweet rose before him and putting her in his coat pocket.

Mary sat the tea in front of him, setting out the cups and saucers while they waited for the kettle to boil over the flames. "Is everything well, your grace. You look a little flushed."

He sat forward, in part to try and disguise his groin, which thankfully was starting to behave itself, but also because he wanted to be closer to her. "I am well, I assure you. Just enjoying my unexpected company."

She smiled at him. The gesture was genuine, and laughter lurked in her eyes. Peter's sister was, if he were to summarize her at all, a jovial, happy kind of woman. She certainly spoke to their guests as if all of them were her friends, and she liked to laugh at jokes, even when Dale didn't find all of those being told by Lord Weston overly amusing.

Dale decided he liked her very much and would like to see her settled and happy and with a gentleman who allowed her to do as she pleased, including rock climbing.

"I am too. When I heard Peter was bringing a duke home this year, I did have a rather unfortunate notion as to what you would be like."

"Really," he said, interested to know what her thoughts may have been. His, upon seeing her the first time, were less than complimentary, and he was ashamed of what he had thought of her that night. A disaster with very little fashion sense. The woman who sat before him had taken charge of her life, and was unrecognizable to the woman he'd first seen. "Do tell me your thoughts."

Lady Mary grinned, her eyes dancing with mischief. "I actually thought you would be a prig. All lofty airs and looking down your nose at all of us. Even though my father is an earl and Peter is your friend, I couldn't help but wonder if you'd find such house parties, festive and merry to be too tame for you?"

"Ahh," he said, leaning back in his chair and running a hand through his hair. "So you've heard the rumors?"

Her grin increased and Dale found himself smiling. "Are they rumors or statements of fact?" She schooled her features and threw him a penetrating gaze. "Are you really as wild as they say you are? Or is the *ton* mistaken in judging you so wrong?"

Dale wished they were judging him incorrectly, but it wasn't so. So how would he answer such a question without looking like the established rake that, in truth, he was. "The *ton* is not wholly incorrect." He couldn't say more, as it was this conversation was highly inappropriate. To tell Peter's sister that he'd had multiple bed partners, sometimes at the same time, was not what this, this... "Your brother tells me you're three and twenty."

"That is correct." She stood and going over to the fire, picked up a cloth that sat on the mantle and then took the kettle off the boil. She poured the hot water into the tea pot, jiggling it a little before letting it sit to brew.

"How old are you?" she asked in return, meeting his gaze.

"Eight and twenty. Old enough to know that our conversation subject is not appropriate."

She chuckled, deep and teasing and the sound warmed his blood. He shouldn't like her this much or her company. He'd certainly never had this reaction to anyone else before. "Then it is lucky that I'm not appropriate. You only need to ask my family just how inappropriate I can be at times. I'm certainly a little too rough about the edges for most people. As well you've found out."

"I like your rough edges." Dale shut his mouth with a snap. What was he saying! She was his best friend's sister. And from the looks that Peter had thrown at him the other night at dinner he did not want Dale going anywhere near her. Not to mention Lady Mary's family expecting her to make a fine match next Season. He hoped she would not consider him in her pursuit of marriage. He would make a terrible husband for her. With both their independent natures, their life would never be calm and sedate, and she did not possess the biddable nature he'd always wanted in a bride and marriage.

God knows Dale would never tolerate being managed by a bluestocking.

"I daresay we shall be friends, your grace?"

Her statement pulled him from his musings and he nodded. "Of course. I would like to think so."

She leaned forward and poured two cups of tea. "Sugar? Milk?"

"Both please," he replied, having always had a sweet tooth, even when it came to his hot beverages.

Lady Mary passed him the cup, a small delicate saucer beneath the fine china and Dale took the opportunity to touch her gloveless fingers. They were warm, soft and did odd things to his stomach.

"Thank you," he said, leaning back in his chair and taking a well-needed sip.

"If we're to be friends, may I call you by your given name. I would like you to call me Mary."

A little warning voice in his mind told him this familiarity was wrong. That he shouldn't be so lax in manners with such a woman, let alone on a first-name basis, but ignoring his own counsel, he found himself saying, "I would like that. You in turn may call me Dale, or Carlton."

Pleased with herself, she settled back onto her seat, once again tucking her legs beneath her on the chair. "Good, because now that we're familiar friends and you're worldly, I'd like some more advice."

Oh damn it. What had he got himself into now? "It depends on what you ask," he said, caution shadowing his tone.

"I'd like some advice on Lord Weston. I've known him, you see, most of my life, he's our neighbor after all, and since he spends so much time in Town, if I were to marry him, I'd be free to stay here in Derbyshire, close to home and all my favorite places in the world to explore."

A cold hard rock lodged in his gut at the thought of Mary marrying Lord Popinjay who was, in Dale's estimation, worse than himself when it came to his philandering about town. Unlike Dale, Lord Weston did not care what happened to his conquests after he'd had his way. He simply turned his back and moved on. That gentleman loved the chase, loved being the center of attention, and Dale knew right down to his core that he'd never be faithful to Mary.

"On further reflection, I do not believe Lord Weston is

suitable after all." He took a sip of his tea, not missing the flash of annoyance in Mary's eyes. "He's not looking for a wife. He told Peter and myself that only days ago. You should look to Lord Fairchild. He is better suited to your nature."

"Even so," she said, biting her bottom lip. "I'm sure that if I managed to kiss his lordship, he would see that we would suit. And that I'd be no trouble in the marriage."

Dale only just stopped himself from cursing. To marry Lord Weston would mean a marriage possibly worse than his parents' had been. Mary would demand loyalty, respect and freedom. All of those things would be lacking if she married Lord Weston. It would only be a matter of time before she'd realize her mistake that unfortunately she'd have to live with for years to come.

"You will not be kissing Lord Weston or marrying him. He's not for you."

She raised her brow, peering at him with interest. "He's the best situated. His estate is right across the fields, for heaven's sake. And you're wrong also. I will kiss his lordship, if I want. No matter if you think I cannot claim one."

Dale placed his cup of tea on the table before them, leaning forward. "I think he would be a fool if he kissed you. It would give you false hope. If his lordship did kiss you it would only be for his own selfish reasons to dally with you."

She stood, an indignant huff escaping her mouth. "You don't think I'm kissable."

Oh hell no, that was not what he was thinking, especially now that she was all fire and brimstone. If only she knew right at this moment, he wanted to claim her mouth. Kiss her hard and deep, pull her close and have her for himself. "Of course not, but young women such as yourself, an innocent—"

"Oh please, spare me the lecture," she said, cutting him off. "I will prove it to you. Before this house party is over I shall kiss Lord Weston properly and I'm going to tell you all about it, and then you will know what you can do with your thoughts on my age and innocence."

Before he could reply, she flounced out of the lodge, slamming the door behind her. "Bloody hell," he swore. Now he'd gone and pricked her pride. And now he would have to watch her like a hawk so she didn't make a fool of herself with Lord Weston. Who, just like a cat, played with its victim before consuming them. And he was determined Lady Mary would not be anyone's feast.

CHAPTER 7

*M*ary kept away from the Duke over the next couple of days, even though his gaze was on her every second of every day. He was shadowing her, she was sure, ensuring she didn't follow through on her threat to kiss Lord Weston. Not that she'd had a chance to even get close to his lordship since her mama's friend, Lady Hectorville had taken a liking to the young viscount.

Tonight, her Mama had set up a card night for all her guests to enjoy. Mary sat beside Louise at the whist table, and contemplated her cards, all the while aware of the scowling duke who sat beside her. But unlike herself, he was scowling at her not the cards he held in his hand.

Was he so very mad at her for telling him that she would kiss Lord Weston? Why it bothered him she couldn't fathom. Probably a brotherly affection he felt honored to have due to his friendship with Peter. She studied him, trying to make him out. He glanced up from his cards, his dark hooded gaze full of determination and something else lurked in his eyes. What though she couldn't fathom. Her skin prickled with awareness and she glanced back down at the table, feeling unsettled of a sudden.

Louise dealt the last round, and going through the play, luck was on Mary's side and she won the last trick with an ace of hearts, beating the duke's king of hearts. Mary laughed, clapping at her good fortune. She smiled at the duke feeling quite the conqueror. His grace leaned back in his chair, throwing his cards on the table

"Well done, Lady Mary. You've beaten us all."

"Of course, I always get what I want, your grace," she said, wanting him to know she didn't just mean at a game of cards. She glanced about the room, noting that Lord Weston was no longer present. Where had he gone? He had been watching them play.

"Another game, Mary?" Louise asked, shuffling the deck to the best of her ability.

"Not just at the moment, Louise." Mary stood. "If you'll excuse me for a minute."

She started for the door with the plan of saying, should anyone ask, that she was intending to use the retiring room her mama had set up downstairs. Mary came out into the hall and turned toward where the room was located. Her parents' country house was one of the largest in the county, and as a young girl she'd lost count when trying to tally how many rooms there were.

The hall had multiple sconces lighting her way, along with candelabras, the smell of beeswax permeating the air. The Aubusson runner beneath her feet cushioned her every step and she smiled, greeting a couple of ladies that she passed on her way. Arriving at the retiring room door, she continued on. Lord Weston had taken a liking to her father's billiard room and it was possible he was spending some time there.

She came up to the room, and peeked through the door. Candelabras were alight, a well-tended fire burning in the grate, but the room itself was empty. Frowning, she turned about wondering where else he would be. Mary continued on and searched the conservatory, the terrace and all were without a soul.

Maybe he'd returned to the card room. She headed back and taking a short cut, she went through her father's library, and the small office that he used when in need of peace and privacy. This area had not been lit, but knowing the room well she crossed the space toward the other door that led onto a corridor with little trouble.

That's when she heard it. A feminine chuckle followed by a male gasp and heavy panting.

Mary stilled, having never heard such a noise before. She looked into the dark recesses of the room, but with her father's desk sitting paramount in the space, Mary could not see beyond.

Another male gasp. "Yes, just like that. Suck it."

Mary slapped a hand over her mouth to hide her gasp. Why in the world would a man be saying such a thing? And who was he saying it to? With the whispered voices she'd not been able to make out which of her parents' guests were ensconced behind the desk, but certainly two were.

She tiptoed up to the desk and peered over. Mary stumbled back, knocking the chair over that was behind her and with a loud thump, she landed on her bottom.

A muffling curse came from the other side of the room, but Mary didn't bother to wait for them to stand and see her there. She bolted for the door into the library, slamming her father's office door firmly behind her as she ran as fast as she could in silk slippers and a gown that was not made to assist with such physical activity.

Mary left the library, coming into her mama's private parlor and slammed head long into the duke of Carlton.

Again...

His arms wrapped about her and for a second time, they went down, Mary landing on top of him. The duke made an *oomph* sound as he took the brunt of the fall.

This time Mary shuffled off him as fast as she could, determined to leave, to get away from everyone and go to her room. Tears stung her eyes at what a silly little dupe she'd been the past few days. Thinking that Lord Weston might actually be a candidate for marriage. To like what he saw in her and be the first and last man to kiss her properly. Shame washed through her at not trusting herself, at not listening to the duke and allowing the little bit of attention he afforded her these past days to give rise to hopes that marriage to a man who suited her character was a possibility.

She was a fool.

"Mary wait," the duke said, catching up to her and pulling her to a stop. "You're upset. What has happened."

At that very moment Lord Weston and Lady Hectorville ran into her father's library, both Mary and the duke turned to look at them. They were still disheveled but at least dressed. Heat bloomed on Mary's cheeks, and she turned her back on them. She could hear Lord Weston start toward them, but the duke moved away, slamming the parlor room door closed and cutting them both off. The snip of the lock echoed in the room before a comforting arm came about her shoulder, leading her toward a nearby chair.

"You need not tell me what you saw, I only needed to look at them to know what has happened. Do you wish for me to tell your parents of Lord Weston's and her ladyship's actions?"

Mary shook her head, shamed that a part of her, the other

part of her that was not affronted or shocked by what she saw, was also a little curious. Jealous even. Were men and women able to do such things to each other? If they were, she'd never known of it.

"No, your grace, that won't be necessary." She stood, throwing him a small smile. He continued to sit, glancing up at her and blast it all he was so handsome. With his strong jaw and chiseled cheekbones, he was an English Adonis.

Before her sat one of the most sought-after gentlemen in England, and just like the rest of them, Mary was always the good-natured friend, always to be sidelined as the dependable, intelligent sister to the future Earl of Lancaster. Never a lady to seek out, to court, and possibly steal a kiss or two from. Oh no, she was too much of a wallflower, a bluestocking to be seen as anything else than that. "Thank you for your concern, but I think I shall retire to my room. I do not feel like socializing any longer today."

Mary left without another word, and just as she expected the duke did not try and stop her. And why would he? He didn't look at her as anything but a friend. A woman to respect but little else.

It seemed to be the story of her life and she was sick of it.

👑

The eve of the Mistletoe Ball arrived with a deluge of snow, but even with the chill of the outdoors, it could not dampen the excitement from the house guests over the festive ball.

Dale stood at the side of Lord and Lady Lancaster's ballroom and watched Lord Weston flounce about like the little peacock that he was. The bastard having been caught with Lady Hectorville, his front falls still gaping from being open, left little imagination as to what he'd been doing with her ladyship. Dale didn't even need to ask Mary what she'd seen.

That the poor girl had harbored feelings toward Lord Weston was unfortunate. The man wouldn't give the chit a second glance. Too opinionated and if Dale was correct, Mary would be too intelligent for such a prick, and the gentleman was too thick to know it. With his own self-importance, that was one trait Dale knew Lord Weston wouldn't tolerate in a bride.

Still, Mary didn't deserve to be taught this lesson in the way that she had been, and he would ensure he sought her out tonight and danced with her.

A little tittering went through the sea of guests and Dale cast his eye across the room, trying to see what everyone was in a little fuss about.

He felt his mouth gape and he closed it with a snap. "Damnation," he muttered, remembering to breathe. His eyes feasted on Lady Mary as she walked into the room. How had she remained hidden for so long when there was such a beauty under all those atrocious gowns her mother had made her wear? More worrying perhaps, was how on earth he'd missed seeing such a prize.

Tonight Mary sparkled like a rare diamond amongst paste.

Arm in arm with her closest friend Louise, she walked through the guests, welcoming and smiling as was her nature. Dale watched as she passed Lord Weston and Lady Hectorville, pleased to see she refused to be lured into conversation, even though the prig Lord Weston still tried, even after his shameful actions that she had happened upon.

The thought made Dale hate him even more and under no circumstances would he allow his lordship to touch one hair on her dark, pretty head.

The man who won Lady Mary's heart would be worthy of her affections. As her brother's best friend, he would ensure that was so, and guarantee that Peter too followed this rule. A rarity such as Mary should not marry anyone who did not deserve her.

Dale narrowed his eyes, the thought of her married to someone else, laughing and enjoying herself as she now was, did not fill him with pleasure. If anything, it soured his mood. He rubbed a hand across his jaw, unsure of why it unsettled him so.

"My sister is a success, it would seem," Peter said, coming up to Dale and pulling his gaze from her.

He nodded, schooling his features. "It would seem she is. I would warn you to keep her from Lord Weston however. I think his lordship has other ideas when it comes to marriage."

They glanced toward the gentleman in question and Dale was glad Peter saw Lady Hectorville slide her hand along Lord Weston's arm, their level of acquaintance obvious to anyone who'd enjoyed such house party games themselves.

"I see," Peter said. "I will mention my concern to father, but as for Mary, well, she doesn't seem to know that his lordship is even here." Peter nodded toward the ballroom floor. "What are your thoughts on Lord Fairchild? He would certainly make a good husband for her. He's titled, a good sort of fellow who doesn't partake in anything notorious, and he has a Scottish hunting lodge even though he hails from Kent. Good game in the highlands."

Dale turned his attention back to Mary who danced a minuet with Lord Fairchild. Her smile lit up the room and their ease of enjoyment together was clear. Mary's face as she looked up at his lordship with something akin to enthrallment and his lordship's was similarly pleased.

A cold knot lodged in his gut. "I know little of him, but I've not heard anything that would cause concern either," Dale said, knowing if he darkened the gentleman's name Peter would listen and would not allow his sister to be courted by him. But Dale could not act with such dishonor. He made a point of relaxing, unfisting his hands at his side. "He looks rather smitten if I'm honest," Dale said instead. "Lady Mary may not need another Season after all."

Peter nodded, then clapped him on the back. "I'm ashamed to say a few days ago I acted atrociously toward you."

"In what way?" Dale thought over their conversations and couldn't remember anything offensive.

"I practically warned you off my sister, albeit not directly, but I feel that you may have believed that to be the case. I hope I have not offended you. Blame it on sibling protectiveness, and know that I believe my concern to be an absurd notion."

Dale glanced at Peter sharply. "Why was it an absurd notion?"

Peter raised his brow, his eyes full of mirth. "Because you would never look at Mary in such a way. She's not your usual type for a start and well, she may have scrubbed up better than any time before this evening, but by tomorrow she'll be back to her normal bluestocking, wallflower self and all this will be forgotten."

Dale turned back to watch the dancers, one in particular whose infectious laughter made his lips twitch. If only that were true. Dale had come to realize that for several days now, even before if he were honest with himself, his attention often lingered on Mary. He was keenly aware whenever she entered a room or when he saw her somewhere in the house, busy with her own pursuits.

Of all the guests here for the Christmas celebrations, Mary was by far the most interesting. And now with her newly found fashion sense, she was blossoming into a beautiful woman, comfortable with who she was, no matter whom she conversed with. She now allowed gentlemen admirers to court her and not be so cold and aloof and it made the little rough pebble she once was, sparkle into a diamond.

Not that Peter needed to know his thoughts. If their friendship was to survive, he would have to get over his growing admiration of his friend's sister and find another lady to occupy his time and attentions.

"Of course you are right. When it comes to your sister, she is quite safe with me." Unable to tear his eyes away from her, he drank in the vision of perfection she was. As if sensing his scrutiny, she glanced up and their eyes met. Held.

A tremor of awareness ran over him, as if she'd recognized the lie he'd just told and was calling him out on it. Within a moment she turned her attention back to Lord Fairchild and he clenched his fist at his side before excusing himself and leaving the ballroom.

He could not want Lady Mary. He ground his teeth, heading for the card room set up in Lord Lancaster's library for the evening, in need of a small respite. He needed to get a grip on his attraction for the chit who he reminded himself, was not what he wanted.

He'd spent his whole childhood on tenterhooks with his parents arguing, he would not have a marriage where the woman might question his decisions and argue with him. Not that he could ever be violent toward a woman, but in the heat of an argument, he also knew he'd not had the best role models on how to go about such matters. The risk was too high.

He stood at the Faro table with Lord Lancaster and two

other gentlemen he'd never met before, ready to lose blunt if it meant he'd forget the jewel out on the dance floor.

He would take out his frustrations here instead of with Lady Mary, where if he were able, he'd give her the first proper kiss she craved, and enjoy every blasted moment of it too.

CHAPTER 8

*M*ary left the ballroom after dancing with as many gentlemen as the time allowed before supper was called. With everyone taking repast in the dining room, she took the opportunity to leave for a moment's peace.

While she'd enjoyed the gentlemen who paid court to her this evening, Lord Fairchild in particular, the very one whom she'd hoped to dance with most had been absent.

She walked past the library and glancing inside could not see the Duke of Carlton anywhere. So where was he? He'd not come back into the ballroom after she'd seen him during her first dance, and after settling her mama down in the dining room for supper she knew he hadn't crept in there either.

Mary checked the usual haunts that gentlemen ventured to during such balls and parties, but the billiard room was empty and so too was the conservatory, so he wasn't having a midnight tryst with anyone.

The idea made the pit of her stomach clench. She pushed the image aside, not wanting to imagine the duke with anyone. She paused at the threshold of a small parlor that was rarely used during the winter months due to its position and lack of sunlight throughout the day.

At least in here she could have a moment alone and regain her composure and remind herself that if she had set her cap for the duke it was only because he'd been so kind to her after finding her in distress over Lord Weston.

A gentleman such as he would never look at a woman such as herself. He was her friend, yes, but she was deluding herself if she thought anything further could come of that friendship.

Mary pushed open the door and the slither of light from the passage illuminated the lone figure sitting on the chaise staring at the unlit hearth before him.

"Your grace," she said, coming into the room and closing the door. "Is everything well? You're sitting in here in the dark."

He turned and watched her; his dark hooded eyes hard to read in the shadowy room that was only somewhat illuminated by the moonlight coming in through the windows.

"You should not be in here alone with me, Mary."

His voice sounded annoyed and she bit her lip. Maybe they were not friends after all, and she'd imagined wrong when she thought they were.

"Apologies, your grace. I shall leave you." She turned for the door, hating the fact that her eyes smarted with rejection.

"Wait," he said as her hand clasped the door handle.

Mary turned but didn't venture to speak.

He stood, watching her with an intensity that sent a shiver of awareness down her spine. Just as it did when she was dancing earlier with Lord Fairchild and she'd caught the duke watching her. He looked displeased seeing her then and she couldn't help but wonder at it. Couldn't help but hope that it might mean he didn't like seeing her dance with anyone but himself.

The duke ran a hand over his jaw, seemingly struggling with some inner turmoil.

"Have you received your proper kiss yet?"

She started, having not expected him to voice such a question to her. "Would you care or even wish to know if I had, your grace? Do you not have other concerns more taxing on your mind than whether I've been kissed or not?"

"It ought to not concern me," he said, with a disgruntled air. "But it does."

What did that mean? Mary walked slowly toward the duke. She couldn't gauge his mood, but the way he stood before her, as if he were almost scared of her and would take flight at any moment, made her bolder than she'd normally be.

"To answer your question, no, I have not kissed anyone, but the night is young, and I seem to have caught the attention of a few eligible gentlemen this evening. Maybe my luck is changing," she teased.

His grace frowned.

"You would throw yourself at anyone?"

Mary gasped. "Excuse me?" she said, shocked that he'd say such a thing to her. She wasn't a wanton hussy. "Jealousy does not suit you, your grace." The moment the words left her lips she regretted them. Of course he wasn't jealous, he was merely looking out for his friend's sister. Didn't wish for her to make a spectacle or fool of herself.

He stepped closer and his chest brushed hers. Mary licked her lips, liking the feel of him touching her there. Perhaps there was a part of her that wanted to act a little wild, rail against the cage of conformity that she was obliged to abide in life.

Her love of the outdoors, doing things only men would

normally take part in and should not exclude the fairer sex. Why should women always do as they're told, toe the line and behave? Not cause a scandal. Why couldn't her husband love her with a passion that suited her spirit?

"If I were to kiss you, Lady Mary, I fear that I should ruin all future kisses you should receive from other suitors, or even that of your future husband."

His words spiked her temper and boldly she lifted her hand, running it down the lapel of his coat. The superfine material was soft to the touch, and yet beneath it lay a bed of hardness, a beating heart that even she could feel was racing beneath her palm.

"Perhaps it will be I who'll ruin all future kisses for you, your grace. I may be an untried miss, but I'm a quick study."

*D*ale stared down at the little hellion before him, her sweet face beguiled, tempting him like no other had before and he ground his teeth, wondering if he should kiss her and damn well prove his point that she'd never have a better instruction in the art with anyone else. He leaned down, but a feather separating their lips. This close she smelled as divine as she looked, a tempting little morsel just waiting to be gobbled up.

"Would you like me to kiss you, Mary?" He used her given name and didn't miss the pleasure that flooded her face.

Her hand, that was still lodged firmly on his chest, slid up over his shoulder to wrap about his neck. The action brought her up hard against his chest, and through the thin silk of her gown all her delectable womanly assets pressed against him.

Her action robbed him of the opportunity to shock her a little, make her turn and run out of here. Instead, she'd met his taunt and upped the stake with a move that left him reeling.

Dale instinctively wrapped his arm about her waist, settling her snug against him and catching her gaze, now heavy with need and expectation, there was little left in him to refuse her wish.

He sealed his lips against hers, but she didn't kiss him back, and her innocence in taking part in such pastimes should've been like a dose of cold water, that had him setting away and keeping her safe.

She was a maid after all. Untried and his best friend's sister. A woman who should've been well and truly off limits.

His wits however, had other ideas.

Instead, he clasped her jaw, tilting her face to meet his kiss better and tempted her with small, soft brushes of his lips against hers. She opened on a sigh and he took the opportunity to delve between her lips, touching her tongue with his.

A sound of utter pleasure emanated from her and he groaned as she mimicked his actions, her own tentative tongue sliding against his.

"Damn it, Mary," he muttered, clasping her jaw with both hands. He stared at her, beseeching her to run. She licked her bottom lip and all sense fled. Muffling a curse, he took her lips again and kissed her. Hard. She met his onslaught head-on, a quick study she certainly was, and her ability to take charge, turn the tables on him and send him reeling when she nipped his lip with a teasing air coiled heat through his veins.

And then she was gone, wrenching herself out of his arms and staring at him with confusion. Her eyes were large and round, her breasts heaving with each breath. Dale glanced at her lips, bruised and swollen from their kiss and his need doubled. She was a temptress and he wanted her. So. Damn. Much.

He wasn't sure what was going through her mind, but whatever it was sent her packing and she ran from the room. Dale swore, running a hand through his hair. He'd over-stepped his mark, perhaps even insulted her. As for what Peter would say to him if he found out...

"Shit," he muttered, striding to the door.

Dale returned to the ball, and keeping to the edges of the room, he spied Mary with her friend, both of them chatting amicably within a small group of men and women both. He studied her a moment, relieved to see she'd not fallen into a fit of the vapors, if anything, she seemed alight with color, her cheeks reddened and her lips still a little swollen from their kiss.

He let out a relieved sigh. He would ask her to dance and ensure she wasn't upset with him and to confirm she was well. After all, they had become somewhat friends the past few days and he would hate his lapse in gentlemanly behavior to sever that.

"How fetching Lady Mary is this evening. What say you, old boy," Lord Weston said, siding up to him, his gaze fixed on Mary.

"Lady Mary always looks well no matter what day it is." Dale didn't like the fact that the man was so vain that his eye was only turned when a woman was up to his standards. Not that Dale was totally innocent of that charge either, he'd certainly thought Mary's wardrobe could do with a little updating.

Lord Weston threw him a curious glance before saying, "I wanted to apologize for the other day how you and Lady Mary found me and Lady Hectorville in a certain state of *déshabillé*. Not my finest moment, but, well, she is a vixen as you well know."

Dale understood what he was saying about her ladyship and her bed sport, but the simple fact that she often shared her bed with many and was never tied to one man soon made it clear to Dale that he could not carry on a liaison with her. He didn't share well, never had, not even as a child.

"It is probably wise that you cease such activity under Lord Lancaster's roof. I don't believe he'd be pleased if he heard Lady Mary was submitted to such an education."

Lord Weston paled at Dale's words and he inwardly laughed. Good. He wanted the fop to feel uneasy. He'd certainly made Mary so.

"Mary won't say anything, she's in love with me, you know. Tried to kiss me the other evening." Lord Weston glanced at Mary now dancing with Lord Fairchild again, and his eyes narrowed in thought. "Maybe I should let her try again and see where it takes us."

Dale fisted his hands at his side. A cold chill swept down his spine and he turned to face the little snot. "You meddle with her and I'll meddle with you. Do you understand?" His voice brooked no argument and was laced with deadly promise.

"What is it to you what I do with Lady Mary?" Lord Weston smirked. "It's not like you wish to court her. Hell, no one has these past five Seasons. She doesn't know this, but we dubbed her Ribbon Rebellion, being so fond of such adornments on her gown and that she's a bit of an unorthodox chit when it comes to society's expectations for her sex. What a laugh we had of it and she was never the wiser. Even Peter had no idea and we even mentioned the name right under his nose." His lordship laughed.

Dale clocked him one in the nose and watched with great satisfaction as he fell like an old, rotten oak, landing on his arse on the parquetry floor. The music stopped and guests standing nearby gasped as Lord Weston tumbled to the ground, blood spurting from his nose and dripping down onto his perfectly tied cravat and waistcoat.

"What the hell do you think you're doing, Carlton?" he said, his voice muffled behind his hands.

Dale leaned over him, pulling out his handkerchief and dropping it on Lord Weston's chest. "Knocking you on your arse just as you deserve. Speak again in front of me, or anywhere else about Lady Mary," he said, lowering his voice, "and you'll get another one."

He walked off, heading for the terrace where he needed to cool off. Five minutes out in the crisp, winter air was just what he needed. Distantly he heard Peter call out for the music to commence and looking over his shoulder he watched as Lady Hectorville helped Lord Weston to his feet, even if the blaggard threw off her support once he stood.

What an ass.

Dale reached the end of the terrace and looked out over the gardens covered in snow, a smile spreading across his face. What fun that was, and not a more deserving bastard was ever on the receiving end of such a blow. It would certainly give the gossips some fodder during the break in the Season and possibly into the new one. Unless another scandal broke before that.

He started when a small gloved hand wrapped about his. He didn't need to turn to know who was beside him.

👑

*M*ary clasped the duke's hand and came to stand before him. He was upset, that was obvious. One only had to look at Lord Weston's swelling nose to know the punch the duke had afforded him had been no light touch.

"What happened?" she asked, not wanting to bother with

77

small talk. She'd seen the duke and Lord Weston talking as she danced and had not missed Lord Weston's amused smirk at her as he talked with his grace. Something told her his lordship's bloody nose had something to do with her.

He stared down at her, and a ripple of heat, not due to the brisk outside air, stole across her skin at his intense gaze. Instead of answering her, he clasped her jaw and took her lips in a searing kiss.

She melted into him, having thought of nothing else from the moment she'd left him earlier in the night. To stay, to kiss the duke was all that she'd wanted to do, but by doing so she courted scandal. Her parents expected her to always show decorum, but she'd never been very good at that, so a stolen kiss or two couldn't hurt surely.

And it did not. It didn't hurt at all. The kiss went on, his mouth hot and insistent against hers, the slight roughness from the stubble on his face marking her skin. Mary wanted to feel more of him. She reached around, wrapping her hands on the inside of his coat, the corded muscles on his back, flexing as he held her close.

She gasped as a hardness pushed against her abdomen. Her stomach clenched. Mary stood on her tiptoes and pressed against him to where she ached most, undulated her hips to feel him better. The duke moaned, hoisting her higher, one hand reaching down to lift her leg around his hip. The cold stone of the balustrade met her bottom as he angled her over the railing, using its support to press harder against her core.

Relentlessly he rubbed against her and it was too much and yet not enough. Liquid heat pooled between her legs and she gasped through the kiss as his actions teased and taunted her toward a pinnacle she could not reach.

A loud, barking laugh from inside made them start and the duke stepped back, looking over his shoulder to ensure they were still alone. They were, and Mary wanted nothing more than to be there. To be alone with the duke and see where that delectable little action would eventually lead.

"Apologies, Lady Mary. I'm heartily ashamed of myself."

Mary couldn't stop her lips from twitching at his embarrassment. She wasn't embarrassed at all. Curious and aching yes, but embarrassed, absolutely not.

She came up to him, running one hand across his jaw. "I'm not," she said, walking back toward the terrace doors and leaving the duke shocked and still behind her.

The words that she wanted to kiss the duke again should shock her, but all she felt right at this moment was expectation. She liked him, more than she'd thought she would and ever since she'd run into him in the conservatory in all truthfulness, she'd hardly thought about Lord Weston.

Oh yes, she may have told the duke she wanted his lordship to kiss her, but that was really only because the duke didn't wish her to. Only one gentleman occupied her mind and he was on the terrace where she'd left him. She'd not thought to meet a man that not only showed interest in her life, the things she loved to do, but also listened, not just nodding and agreeing for propriety's sake.

Oh no, now that she'd had a small taste of what his grace could do to her, he wasn't going to escape that easily. And with a few days left of the house party, she would have to come up with a plan to make him lose such steadfast control about her again and kiss her some more. The idea flittered through her mind that the duke might ask for her hand and nerves pooled in her belly. She bit her lip, not wanting to give rise to hope when realistically a few stolen kisses did not mean he would offer marriage. Even so, the thought of spending more time with his grace, of kissing him yet again made excitement thrum through her veins. What a wonderful thought indeed.

CHAPTER 9

*O*ver the next few days Dale fought to keep his distance from Lady Mary, but everywhere he turned she seemed to be there. Her newfound popularity ensured a bevy of gentlemen guests always surrounded her. Her smile and intelligent conversations about politics, horses or fishing, had kept them coming back for more, and there was little doubt in his mind that come next Season she would be snatched off the marriage mart merry-go-round that so many got stuck on.

He sat on a chaise longue, reading the latest news from London. The snow was falling heavily and it was Christmas Eve meaning everyone was indoors, keeping themselves occupied with cards or music. Earlier that day Dale had played a game of billiards with Peter, but the arrival of Lord Weston, his nose still bruised from the other evening, soon meant he'd excused himself.

The little popinjay had not taken his warning to heart and continued to seek out Lady Mary at any opportunity. No doubt just to vex Dale, and vexing him, it most certainly was.

Dale looked over the top of his paper and watched Lord

Weston enter the front parlor. Mary was busy reading a book in a nearby chair. It was only the two of them, and she'd tucked her legs beneath her gown like she had done in the hunting lodge. A relaxed pose that he would assume a married couple might have if relaxed within each other's company.

Lord Weston sat across from her, and Dale watched as she settled herself in a more appropriate fashion, talking politely to his lordship, but if Dale was any judge of character, he would guess her interest had cooled toward his lordship.

She glanced at him and his suspicions were confirmed. The heat and determination he read in her eyes were all for him, and not the dandy sprouting on about waistcoats before her.

If Lord Weston noticed her inattention he didn't seem to say, just continued to speak as if he had a captive audience.

Dale's lips twitched. How wrong he was.

Not for anything could he tear his gaze away. The more he looked, the more he wanted to see of her, not just across the room, but elsewhere too. Someplace quiet, private and alone. Asleep on his bed would also do very well.

Peter stood before him, cutting off his view. Dale started and looked up, schooling his features. His friend stared down at him with something akin to annoyance and Dale gritted his teeth. "Morning Peter," he said, folding his paper and setting it on his lap.

"We need to talk."

His friend's concerned tone made him frown. "Sit and tell me what is troubling you."

Peter did as Dale asked and he gave his friend his full attention. "Lord Weston has asked Father if he may court Mary."

Dale sat up, fury spiking through him at the audacity of the man after he'd told him to stay the hell away from her.

"I have not forgotten your warning about him, and I told my parents of your concern, but they're adamant that Lord Weston is genuine and whatever you saw his lordship and Lady Hectorville doing was wholly innocent."

Dale swore. "Peter, your sister caught them in a compromising position, not I. I merely was the messenger. She cannot marry him; he'll never be faithful to her and she deserves so much more than that."

Peter's mouth pulled into a thin, disapproving line. "I agree. We must help her find a gentleman who is suitable." His friend turned to him. "Do you have any ideas?"

Dale pulled at his cravat, the warmth of the room making him sweat. "No-one present. I think she needs to have her Season next year and see if there are any more suitable gentlemen who pay court to her." He paused, glancing at her. Lord Weston had shuffled closer to her person. If he moved any closer, he'd be sitting on Mary's lap.

"If your parents will not listen, we'll have to ensure Lord Weston gets the message loud and clear to stay away. He'll end up giving her a disease."

Peter's eyes flew wide and he gasped. "Surely you jest."

Dale shrugged, partly wondering why he was so set on Lady Mary not being married to such a bastard. What was it to him whom she married? So long as she was happy with her choice, he really didn't have much say in the matter. But to think of her married to another, to share her bed, to have her bestow delectable kisses to anyone but him... He glared at Lord Weston, not appreciating the thought.

"I do not. With the amount of bed-fellows he's had, it'll only be matter of time before she has the pox."

Peter stood, and Dale watched as Mary's brother marched up to Lord Weston asking him to a game of billiards. Dale picked up his newspaper, feigning reading as he listened to the conversation. That Peter had surmised that if he kept Lord Weston away from Mary that would ensure the chap would not court her.

It was basic in concept, but could work, especially if Dale helped him with that endeavor. He smiled knowing he'd enjoy hindering Lord Popinjay from being able to pay court to Mary.

A lone finger pulled his paper down and Dale looked up to see Mary standing before him. Her gown had a pretty light green floral pattern over it. It was summery in appearance, but with the long sleeves and green shawl it was suitable for the cold time of year.

"Lady Mary," he drawled, his body alerting to the fact that she was so close to him. Her hand picked up his paper and tossed it on the seat beside him. She leaned down, placing her hands on either side of his head, pushing him back into the cushion.

"What are you and my brother up to? Lord Weston was trying to court me and you should know I was enjoying it very much."

"As if you could marry such a man."

She raised one brow, a small grin on her lips. "No, of course not, but I was enjoying watching you dislike his courting. That, your grace, was worth the few minutes in his presence."

Dale reached out, running a finger down the small hollow at the front of her throat, tracing it down between her breasts, which at this angle, spilled a little over the front of her gown. He bit back a groan, itching to spread his hand over her soft silken skin, tease the sweet nipples to hardened peaks beneath her dress.

"Don't push me, Lady Mary. You may not like the outcome."

She chuckled, leaning down further to kiss him softly on the lips. He didn't move for fear of ripping her down on the seat beside him and finishing what they'd started the other night. The memory of her pliant body, willing and enjoying him on the terrace filled his mind and his body hardened. They were in the front parlor damn it; anyone could come in at any moment. He glanced quickly toward the door and clenched his hands at his side when he realized it was open.

"Maybe I'd like the outcome," she said, running a finger over his bottom lip before standing up and severing all contact. The instant she was gone he missed her touch. He swallowed, completely at a loss as to how he was to handle the little vixen. Never had he met a woman who threw the rules of society aside to walk her own special path through life.

He was utterly beguiled.

Giving him another saucy smile at the door, she turned and left the room. He stared after her, his heart racing in his chest as if he'd been taking part in strenuous exercise.

If only he were, and with Lady Mary, now that would make an enjoyable afternoon.

*L*ater that night Mary stood speaking with Louise in the upstairs drawing room, a sprig of mistletoe in her hand. She would not normally be so bold as to carry around the little plant that would allow her to kiss anyone she choose, but she was determined to further acquaint herself with the duke.

He was simply too irresistible to ignore, and she wanted to feel all that he made her feel the other night.

"If your mama finds out that you're wishing to steal a kiss from the Duke of Carlton she'll have your head on a platter and serve it for supper. You know they're already irritable with you not making a match last Season."

"That was by choice, Louise. If I had wished for an offer I could've showed two gentlemen that I can think of off the top of my head who would've furthered their acquaintance with me, but it was not what I wanted." In fact, Mary had done everything in her power to thwart suitors. One could not give her heart to a man who was only interested in what you brought to the marriage. That was not who Mary was. She wanted to be able to converse with the man she married, to be on equal footing within their home. If she could not have such outside the walls of her house, then she would damn well have it within it.

"And now you wish the duke to further his acquaintance?" Louise searched her gaze, a small frown upon her brow.

Mary shrugged. "I don't know what I want from the duke, another kiss would be nice," she said, teasing Louise a little. "He's different from anyone I've ever met before I suppose. He doesn't ridicule me for my likes and he actually talks to me, no one ever really talks to you in London or listens for that matter. The gentlemen make out they do, but they really do not."

"And the duke does?" Louise asked, grinning.

Mary nodded. "He does, and it doesn't hurt that his kisses are very nice too." Left her aching in places she didn't even know could ache. She wanted to feel that again.

"You're too wild, Mary." Her friend shook her head, an amused smirk across her lips. "Whatever will your family do with you?"

Mary laughed. "Nothing or perhaps they could lock me up in a convent abroad I suppose, but Papa would never allow that. As much as they may despair at my independent ideas and hobbies, they would never break my heart by punishing me for them."

"That is true." Louise nodded toward the door. "The duke has arrived."

She cast a glance in his direction and watched as he entered with her brother by his side. The two made a striking pair. The duke with his dark hair and coloring and her brother who was all blond and angelic. Both had reputations about London however, the duke more than anyone. A gentleman every debutante wanted and yet none had managed to turn his gaze.

Until now…

He met her stare across the room as they made their way into the throng of guests and the place behind her breast fluttered. Mary watched as he stood beside her brother, quiet and watchful of the room, her more than most, and she couldn't help but wonder what if. What if she was the one to turn the duke's gaze to her and only her. Forever.

Would he make her give up her love of freedom, her desire to do as she wished whenever she chose, her hobbies outside the ballroom. Would he be like so many of the gentlemen of the *ton* who only saw their wives as trophies to be admired, exalted and boasted about, but never anything else.

The thought left her cold and she twisted the mistletoe in her fingers, wondering if she should simply stop teasing the duke and leave him well alone. As it was, the kiss she bestowed on him only yesterday in the drawing room had been a risk, and had her parents or brother walked in and seen her actions the duke would already be her husband. The kiss on the terrace was worse with the ball taking place right beside them. But surely a gentleman who took an interest as he did was not so backward in thinking. Surely he would not wish her to change.

"He appears to watch you a great deal, Mary."

Mary turned and threw the piece of mistletoe into the fire behind them, before sitting on the settee before the hearth. She smiled at Louise. "He's simply watching to make sure Lord Weston does not try and court me. Do not read into his attention any more than that."

"I think you may be wrong about that," Louise said, sitting also. Mary fidgeted with her gown and fought not to look in his direction. An impossibility almost.

Mary set out to enjoy the night of impromptu dancing some of the guests took part in, supper, games and cards. Her mother had ordered made her favorite desserts of lemon cake and ices. Her father wore his silly Christmas hat that had little elves sewn onto it and her mother's festive gown was the deepest shade of red with small sprigs of holly sewed about the hems.

It was times like these with her family that she loved the most, and her eyes smarted that if she married, it would no longer just be the four of them. She would leave to spend such times with her new husband. The gentleman might choose to spend Christmas alone or with his own family. Everything would change.

Out the corner of her eye she watched as the duke sat in a seat across from her and Louise. He crossed his long legs, leaning back in the chair and waited. It reminded Mary of a lion before it pounced on its prey.

The heat of his gaze bore into her until she couldn't take it any longer and she looked at him. He glanced at her with an air of boredom and heat rose on her cheeks at the memory of their time on the terrace. She swallowed, hoping he'd assume the fire had made her warm and not him.

"Did you know that you're sitting under a sprig of mistle-toe, Lady Mary?"

Mary looked up to see a row of holly and mistletoe had

been strung across the room's ceiling directly above where she sat. She cringed. "I did not," she said in a tone that she hoped conveyed boredom and not hope. Louise chuckled and tried to mask it with a cough.

"I'm going to talk to your mama for a moment. I'll be back soon, Mary," she said, standing and leaving her alone with the duke.

Mary fidgeted with her hands in her lap, her attention snapping back to the duke. His eyes ran over her person and she shivered at the heat that banked in his gaze. Desire rushed through her, hot and impatient and she closed her eyes a moment to gain some semblance of control. She shouldn't want to kiss him again, but little else had occupied her mind since they'd done it last. She was turning into a veritable wanton.

How could she ever remain a spinster, a wallflower if she hankered for his touch, his mouth on hers and everything else that he could give her?

"Lord Weston isn't sitting with me, so why are you, your grace?" she asked.

He leaned forward, running a hand over his jaw. He looked up at her and a piece of his hair fell across his eye. It made him look even more wicked than normal and her stomach fluttered. "That, Lady Mary, I have been asking myself and I cannot fathom as to why."

She raised her brow, having not expected him to be so honest. The way he was looking at her, as if she were the tastiest morsel in the room made her question her priorities. She licked her lips, wondering yet again if he would be the type of man who'd ask his wife to change who she was for the sake of the title, of what was expected by the *ton*.

Mary couldn't abide by such a life if that was what he wished. Not that the duke was looking to marry her, but from the hunger she read in his eyes, he was certainly after something.

"Really?" Mary cast a glance about the room, seeing that they were quite alone. "I think I do."

He leaned back in his chair, a grin on his delectable lips that she wanted him to ravish her with. "Do tell," he said, matter of fact.

Never one not to be honest or talk bluntly she studied him a moment. "I think you're here because you want to be. I think you're here because you want to kiss me again," she whispered. "And I think you're here because you are trying to work out why that is the case."

His eyes narrowed, his features cooling a little at her words. "While I will admit that your kiss was very...enjoyable, I'm merely here to keep Lord Weston from approaching you. The cad can find someone else to ruin, it won't be you."

But maybe it'll be you instead... Mary bit her lip, a part of her wanting Lord Weston to enter, to court and make a fuss of her, if only to set off the duke's ire. "If I married Lord Weston I'd always live near my childhood home. I could continue on as I always have in Derbyshire. His lordship could come and go as he pleases and so too could I." Mary leaned forward, knowing she was giving him a little glimpse of her assets. "Perhaps you ought to leave so he can continue his courtship of me. I'm not immune to staying in Derbyshire."

All lies, she was totally immune to Lord Weston's charms, certainly after she saw what he was doing with Lady Hectorville and after she'd kissed the man who sat across from her. The duke's gaze darkened further, and she schooled her features, not wanting him to know she could read him like a book.

CHAPTER 10

*D*ale took a calming breath, not sure if he wanted to shake a little sense into the maddening chit or kiss her senseless. Both, he assumed would do equally well. He'd promised Peter he would keep Mary out of Lord Weston's clutches, but it was another thing entirely to keep her out of his own.

True, she drove him mad, vexed him often with her sharp tongue, and kissed like she'd been taking part in such actions for years, not days. The memory of her in his embrace haunted him nightly, and he'd taken his gentlemanly needs into his own hands. Literally.

He cleared his throat. "You do not need to make any hasty decisions; you have next Season still to attend." Dale drank in the vision of her. The moment he'd seen her tonight, her golden silk gown and emerald necklace gave her a festive air, and his gut had clenched at the beauty she was.

How had he not seen it under all those ribbons and bows. He could only fathom that she'd done all that she could to remain invisible when in Town. That was no longer the case. No gentleman in attendance was unaware of Lady Mary's presence, and the admiring glances, the attention she'd had bestowed on her these past days was proof of that.

Next year she would find a gentleman who suited her and she would marry him.

The thought left him cold.

"If I made my decision now, I would not have to attend London next year. I could stay in Derbyshire." She picked up her glass of wine that sat on a small table beside her chair and took a sip. She met his eyes over the rim of the glass, and he could read the amusement in her green orbs.

What are you playing at minx…?

"And now that you've taught me how to kiss, what sort of passions I would like in a husband, Lord Weston may be open to my eligibility. Lady Hectorville is after all a lot older than himself. I think I'm more suited to him in age."

Anger simmered in Dale's blood and he fisted his hands in his lap. "You would kiss Lord Weston if given the opportunity?"

"Of course," Lady Mary said, shrugging one delicate shoulder. "I kissed you, did I not? I'm three and twenty, more than old enough to know a little of what is to come should I marry. And I must admit that I find kissing very…" she pursed her lips and his body hardened. "Nice."

Dale ground his teeth, having heard enough of Mary kissing anyone she deemed suitable. "Just because Lord Weston is your neighbor here does not make him a suitable candidate. I will not allow you to throw yourself at him."

She stood, and he sat forward as she strode toward him, walked past and ran her hand up his lapels to his shoulder. His body roared with annoyance. She had not agreed to his terms. To her brother's wishes. "You cannot stop me, your grace."

The hell he couldn't. He stood and stormed after her. He followed her into a nearby corridor that ran off the library, it was unlit and the bare wooden floors gave rise to it only being used by servants.

"I will tell your brother what you're playing at, so I can stop you, Lady Mary."

She rounded on him, pushing him hard up against the wall. He stared at her a moment, not quite believing she'd manhandled him in such a way, before all thought fled from his mind when he realized her hand was running down his chest to run across his stomach.

He lay his head back against the wall, watching her take her fill of his body, wishing that her hand would delve lower and wrap about his aching cock.

"Should I tell my brother what you did to me over the terrace railing, your grace? How you made me ache. How you made me crave things I don't even understand? If I'm willing to throw myself at Lord Weston it all could be laid at your door?"

"How so?" he rasped, his voice laced in agony.

"Because," she said, her hand running about his waist to drop lower and cover one cheek of his arse, squeezing it a little. Her lips were just a breath away from his. She smelled of wine and spices. Dale kept his hands locked at his side knowing that if he placed them on her, there would be no turning back with what he wanted to do with her.

"At night the pleasure you wrought inside of me is all that I think about. I want to have that again, and if Lord Weston marries me, then I can have that and everything else as well. My life here as it's always been."

"You do not need to marry to find pleasure." Dale cursed his words, but he could not regret saying them. He wanted her. Wanted to taste and kiss every morsel of her body. Wanted her to shatter under his ministrations.

"And just as you instructed me in the art of kissing, you'll instruct me in that art as well?"

"Hell yes," he said, slamming his mouth against hers. She gasped, and kissed him back with as much fire, as much need as his own. His body was aflame, hot and wanting. He broke the kiss, ignoring her moan of displeasure and looked about. Seeing a door nearby, he pulled her toward it, opening it to find a storeroom housing linen.

Dale yanked her inside, closing the door and snipping the lock.

Before he'd turned back to her, she'd clasped his face and pulled him in for a kiss. A small part of him thought that she'd vexed him on purpose, brought on such a reaction from him. But right at this moment, he didn't care. All he cared for was that she was in his arms and his to have.

He backed her up toward a small table and lifting her quickly he sat her atop it. For a moment he watched her, both of their breathing was ragged, her breasts rising and falling with each intake of air. In the meagerly lit room, her golden gown was a beacon. Her leg idly swung, her silk slipper falling to the floor and he bit back a groan, knowing what he was about to do to her could never be undone.

Dale kneeled, slipping her other foot free of her shoe. He ran his hand up her long, soft stockinged leg reaching up until he felt the ribbon about her garter. Untying it, he slipped one and then the other off her leg, unable to stop himself from leaning forward and kissing her inner thigh, her knee, her sweet, delicate ankle.

Her fingers spiked through his hair, and he looked up, meeting her gaze. Her eyes were wide, hungry, her face flushed with anticipation and perhaps a little discomfiture. She had no reason to be so. He'd never do anything to hurt or embarrass her.

He gathered the hem of her gown and slowly slid it up her legs and prayed she would not stop him.

ⱮⱮ

*M*ary shook all over, her body thrumming with expectation and wonder over what the duke was about to do to her. She had goaded and teased him into acting out in such a way, but the idea she could find pleasure without losing her innocence was an opportunity she would never pass up.

He pushed her legs apart, leaving her vulnerable, and causing her to lean back on her hands. Heat bloomed on her cheeks but she could not look away, for she was mesmerized by what he was doing to her. He bestowed an open mouth kiss on her inner thigh, hot and wet. The action was so private, a ministration that she'd never thought a man would ever do to a woman. Mary gasped, biting her lip, uncertain of what he meant to do from this point on.

"Lie back," he commanded, his voice a gravelly purr. The duke stood and pushed her to lay flat on the table. A stack of linens lay beneath her head and she gasped as cool air kissed higher on her leg, before her gown pooled at her waist.

His large hands slid over her abdomen, her thighs, before pushing her legs further apart. His hot breath above her most private of places warmed her, and then he was there, his mouth, his tongue, teasing, flicking and kissing her as he had against her mouth.

Mary reached down, clasping his hair, holding him to her and pushing away the little voice that shouted at her to stop. That this was not appropriate or becoming for a lady. But she no longer cared. All she cared was that his mouth was on her and whatever he was doing to her felt so perfectly delicious.

He clasped the underside of her legs and lifted them to sit on his shoulders. Pushing forward, he flicked her with his tongue, before she felt him run a finger down over her core, teasing her entrance.

Mary moaned having never felt anything so wickedly good before in her life.

"You taste so damn sweet," he said, meeting her gaze as he pressed one finger slowly into her.

She bit her lip, wanting to scream at the pleasure of his touch. Instead she clenched around his finger, milking it and wishing there was another part of him that could fill and inflame her.

He teased her relentlessly for some minutes. It was all too much, but not enough. And then she was there, a pinnacle worth the climb and one she wanted to fall from again and again.

She gasped as pleasure coursed through her, and all the while the duke did not let up. He continued to pull and tease every last drop of bliss from her he could. Her muscles felt spent and weak and she sighed, smiling a little as he stood and helped right her gown, her stockings and the silk slippers that had fallen onto the floor.

"You look positively ravished."

Mary sat up, leaning on her elbows. "And you, your grace look like you're in pain." She sat all the way up, flattening out her gown and checking that her hair was reasonably tidy. Running a hand over his jaw, she touched his lips, heat coursing through her with the knowledge of what they could do to her.

She shook her head. "I had no idea that a man's mouth could be so very clever."

He smiled, chuckling and stepping between her legs, his hardened member hard up against her own sex. She clutched at his lapels, fire coursing through her once again.

"You might be surprised just how very clever I am." He kissed her and she could taste her own tartness. Such a thing should revolt her, but instead, she drank him in, loving the fact that he'd held no such remorse in bringing her pleasure while leaving her a maid.

She broke the kiss. "Tell me how I can please you."

His nostrils flared and he stepped back, severing the contact. "It is enough that you did this evening. We need not do any more."

He walked to the door and opened it a little, looking out into the hall. "There is no one about. You should return to the parlor or head to your room. I shall make an appearance and then retire myself."

Mary shuffled off the folding table, checking that the linens behind her were as they had been when they entered the room. She came up to him, trying to gauge what he was thinking. What he thought of her and what they'd done. "Even with what happened in here tonight I do not want you to think that I expect anything from you. Marriage is not an institution that I want unless I'm certain I've chosen correctly, so please do not allow any gentlemanly honor to raise its head and insist that you make an honest woman of me."

Something flickered in his eyes, relief, regret, that she couldn't tell. He leaned down, kissing her lips and the action felt almost final. Like he was drawing a line beneath them and finishing the little liaison in his life.

"I'm glad you do not expect such a thing, Lady Mary, for as you know I also do not wish to be saddled with a wife, not for some time yet. I do not wish to give you false hope of something more even though I should after what I just did to you."

She shivered at the reminder, her body wanting more of him. At least in this respect. "Then we're in agreement," she said, tapping his cheek with the palm of her hand before moving past him and leaving him in the linen closet. Mary started toward her room, not wanting to face anyone, and feeling as though they had both lost a sweet opportunity that was not offered to everyone in life.

Making her room, she entered and shut the door, stifling a yelp when she found Louise sitting on the chair before the fire. "Oh, you're back. I wondered where you got off to. Your mama was looking for you and I said I'd come and check on you thinking you'd be in your room. But you were not." Louise threw her a penetrating stare. "Where were you, Mary?"

Heat flamed her cheeks and for a moment she fought to come up with an idea that would quell her friend's suspicions. But at Louise's knowing stare, she knew it was pointless. Louise had always been able to read her like a book.

"I was with the Duke of Carlton. In a linen closet. Alone."

Louise's eyes flared in alarm, her mouth gaping like a fish out of water. "And were you talking to the duke in this closet?"

Mary sat across from her, pulling her legs up beneath her gown. "Oh yes we talked a great deal. He in fact used his mouth a lot." Heat infused her face at the memory of his wicked mouth that even now her body craved to feel again.

"Be careful, Mary," Louise said, her tone serious. "Or you'll end up married before the New Year, nevertheless the next Season. I didn't think you wanted a husband at all. Too stifling and controlling for your nature."

All true, husbands had always brought forth an idea of selfish, lazy obnoxious beings who would tell her what to do and when. What to wear and how to act. And yet, the duke had not dismissed her lifestyle, or thought it was unbecoming of a woman. Perhaps the duke, as high and mighty as he was, was in fact not so very stuffy after all. He could perchance be different from all the rest.

"I'm still a maid. There was no indiscretion, Louise, so

please stop looking at me so shocked." Well, there was rather a nice one, but nothing that could ruin her since no one knew of it. Some things should remain private, and her rendezvous with the duke was one of them.

"You spoke of marriage with the duke?"

"Well, actually he brought it up, but only to remind me of the fact that he was not looking for a bride any more than I was looking for a groom. So we're quite in agreement on that score."

The thought left a hollow ache beneath her breast. She liked him, more than anyone else before and they were friends. Intimate ones at that.

But would he suit as a husband? Would he allow her to be who she was? Certainly now that she knew what a man could do for a woman, taking a husband wasn't so foreign to her. The duke certainly had been the first man to ever inspire desire within her, and so she would not discount him too soon, even after what they'd both said downstairs.

She shivered, thinking of his touch, his wicked kisses over her body. Perhaps being married would not be so much of a chore after all. Not if they were all like the Duke of Carlton. And not if she were to continue on as she'd always had when not under the condescending gaze of the *ton*.

CHAPTER 11

*D*ale lay in his bed staring up at the ceiling, the dark winter night as chilled as his own respectability. He should not have touched Mary. Not one strand on her pretty dark-haired head.

His cock stirred at the thought of her beneath him, writhing and grinding herself against his mouth and he groaned. Damn it. He shut his eyes, willing the torturous memory away, and yet it did not. If anything, it became more vivid, tempting him to leave the room, stride to hers and finish what they'd started.

He'd not traveled to Derbyshire to marry a country chit who was too independent and bossy for his nature. He'd always pictured a nice docile woman by his side when the time came, a blonde goddess with angelic features. The harridan that slept only a few doors from his was the antithesis of all that he'd pictured.

And damn she tempted him. More than any had before.

Dale sighed, his body taut with unsated desire. He forced himself to stay where he was, not to move and seek her out.

To show her more of what a man and woman could do together without compromising her maidenhead.

A slither of light burst into the room as his door opened, before it was closed just as quick. The snip of the lock had him sitting up.

"Who's there?" he asked, trying to focus his eyes on the figure that moved slowly toward his bed.

He inwardly groaned when he recognized who was present. "You need to leave, Margaret. There is nothing in this bed for you."

She came up onto the mattress, a pouty expression on her lips that made her look absurd and a little desperate. "Come Carlton. Let me love you as you like." Her hand slid over his cock and he pushed her hand away, hating the fact that his body roared for release. But he didn't want Margaret beneath him. He wanted the maddening miss who slept down the hall.

Dale pushed away from her, getting off the bed. He clasped her upper arm, pulling her toward the door. "Out. Before someone sees you in here. What we had is long past and I'm sure there are other gentlemen present at this house party who'll welcome you into their beds."

She glared at him, all seduction gone. "You used to be amusing." He unlocked the door, ushering her out. At her little squeak, he looked up and met the shocked gaze of Mary.

♕

*M*ary took a couple of steps backward almost stumbling. "I'm sorry. I'm just on my way downstairs. I left the book I was reading in the library earlier today," she babbled, moving past them, pulling her robe closer about her and ignoring Lady Hectorville's giggle and whispered conversation with the duke about being caught.

What the duke said in reply was lost to Mary as she headed downstairs. That she was actually heading to the duke's room when he'd escorted Lady Hectorville from his company was not what she'd expected to see. Grateful she had been saved from her own foolhardiness she headed toward the library. She went into the library and picked up the first book she could find, an old tome on gardening in England's northern lands.

Mary took a moment to calm her heart. She blinked, breathed in a deep breath to try and halt the tears that blurred her vision. This was why she was not suited to be the wife of any gentleman. They were unfaithful, rotten to the core; people who wanted all and everything without a care as to whom they might hurt in their pursuit of pleasure and vice.

The duke could have at least waited a day before stooping so low to invite her ladyship into his bed. "Bastard," she mumbled. That she'd only parted from his company hours before, that he'd had his hands and mouth on her person the same day as her ladyship left a sour taste in her mouth and a dull ache behind her breast.

The door to the library opened and the duke came in, looking about the darkened space searching for her. Mary didn't move from her place beside the door, not in the mood to help his cause in finding her in any possible manner.

He turned and spied her, shutting the door with a snap. "Mary, let me explain."

She moved away from him, pulling her robe tighter about herself as if to protect her heart. "What I saw was more than self-explanatory, your grace."

He strode over to her, his tall, imposing frame dwarfing her against the bookshelf. "I did not sleep with Lady

Hectorville. She came to my room and I told her to leave. What you witnessed was my ousting of her."

Mary looked up into his eyes and in the moonlight saw the determination there to make her believe him. He was a renowned rogue, rumored in London to have many lovers. Finding him in such a compromising position at a house party would not be out of character, but there was something in his tone that gave her pause. Stopped her from accusing him of being a liar.

"Why should I believe you?" she asked, needing him to tell her that she was wrong in her assumptions and he was being honest. "I've heard the rumors about you and Lady Hectorville. That she was once your lover."

"That was a mistake that I made one night when I was in my cups. I have not made the error again. What you saw just now was me kicking her from my room."

"So you forget often what you do when you're drunk. Shows a certain type of fickleness of character, your grace." She shook her head, hating the fact she'd allowed herself to think that there could be a possibility with him. A future. The duke was no different than every other gentleman in the *ton*. Only out for what they could get, whether it be women or blunt. To be married to a man, allow herself to care for someone who might simply imbibe too much one evening and sleep with someone else was not to be borne. She certainly could not stomach such an insult.

His grace sighed, looking up at the ceiling a moment before meeting her gaze. "I was not married, Mary. The tryst hurt no one. When I marry, I will be true to my wife. *Always*."

Mary crossed her arms over her chest, her stomach in knots over what to believe. What she saw or what the duke was telling her. She had gone to his room after tossing and turning in bed thinking of him, wanting to see him again, be with him and see what else he could show her.

Scandalous behavior and not so different from what the duke and many of their set did every night in London during the Season. She held no hope of marrying the man, so to be so offended and upset seemed a silly reaction to have.

That's because you do hold a little hope the duke will ask for your hand...because you care.

Mary pushed the thought aside, dismissing it. "You don't owe me an explanation, your grace. We're not betrothed."

The muscle in his jaw clenched as he stepped toward her. "I need to explain. You need to understand."

"What?" she asked, meeting his gaze. "What do I need to understand?"

He stepped closer still, his warm, muscled body warming her blood. "You need to understand that the only woman I want in my bed is you."

Mary swallowed, clasping the book against her chest as if it were some lifesaving apparatus. Did his grace really mean that?

He glanced down at the tome in her hand. "Where were you off to really? I would be surprised if your reading desires had turned to gardening in the northern climes of a sudden."

She bit her lip, the need to flee, to save herself rode hard on her heels and yet she could not move away. "I find gardening very interesting and engaging." What on earth was she saying!

"Liar," he whispered, leaning down and clasping her cheeks.

Mary nodded. "Yes. That too."

He took her lips in a searing kiss, lifting her quickly to place her on the bookcase shelf behind her.

"You've been haunting my dreams and waking moments, Mary. Only *you*."

That was said with such an edge of frustration she believed him, and something improper inside of her thrilled.

His height placed him directly at her core and she melted into his arms. All thoughts of Lady Hectorville fled from her mind, of his roguish ways in Town, all of it. The moment he touched her she knew it was right. What she wanted.

His hand slid down to grapple with the hem of her nightgown, the cool night air kissing her legs as he pushed it to pool at her waist. And this time, she would get what she wanted. Him.

CHAPTER 12

*D*ale tried to rein in his overwhelming need for the woman in his arms, but he could not. And if he were honest with himself, unless she said to stop, he'd do all and anything that she wanted.

"Tell me again," she murmured, a sensual, secretive smile about her lips.

He ground against her core, the memory of her sweet lips making him as hard as stone. "I want you and no one else."

Her fingers spiked through his hair, pulling him close. "Yes." Her whispered word snapped the thin thread that he walked along, the one all gentlemen should to keep them from despoiling virginal women set on husbands. Mary might not be interested in husband hunting right at this moment, but her family certainly was and that in itself should give him pause.

But it did not.

The house was deadly quiet, the falling snow outside masking any exterior sounds, and all he could hear was them. A melody that drove him to part her legs, to tease her flesh with his fingers before fumbling with the front of his pants.

Their movements were desperate, quick and full of need. Her fingers clawed into his shoulders, her body slick and hot, ready and willing for what was to come. Dale kissed her with a fervor that left him breathless, he'd never been so desperate to sheathe himself within a woman before, to lose himself and forget everything that impacted his life.

It was simply Mary and him. No-one else and that was enough.

She begged him, her raspy, seductive tone whispering against his lips and he kissed her, deep and sure as he thrust within her. She stilled in his arms and he held himself motionless a moment, waiting for her to adjust to his size.

"I'm sorry," he said, kissing her cheek, her chin and neck, reaching down to run a hand over her breast and sliding her puckered nipple between his thumb and forefinger. She relaxed in his arms, her hands pulling at him in silent want, and he slowly eased out, before thrusting back within her again.

She moaned his name, an elixir that banked a fire burning within him. He took her, laid claim to her body, the slap of skin hitting skin the only sound in the room. Mary didn't shy away from the ferocious way they came together. Being a maid, they should be on the softness of sheets and bedding, taking his sweet time to teach her how to love, to move and take pleasure. Not this way, hard up against a wooden book-case, sneaking about in the quiet of the night. Part of him registered the shame of taking her so and he cringed.

"Dale," she gasped, her legs high against his hips. She watched him as he pumped relentlessly into her hot core until at last she lay her head back against the cupboard and let go.

He smothered her cry of release with a kiss, her tight core

milking him of his own pleasure. Dale slumped against her, their breathing ragged and his ability to move, to pull out of her and set them to rights lost on him a moment.

Her legs went limp and he pulled back, helping her off the bookcase and to stand. Righting her nightgown and his own breeches which shamefully he'd not even removed, had simply ripped open at the front. He pulled her into a kiss, needing to hold her in his arms, to taste her sweetness on his lips.

The door flew open and they pulled apart as if they'd been burned. Dale steeled himself as the furious Peter and Lord Lancaster stared at him, murder most clearly on their mind.

Dale glanced behind his lordship to the stairs leading to the first floor and didn't miss Lady Hectorville turning toward her room, a self-satisfied smirk on her face.

"You had better have a good explanation as to why you're both down in the library in the middle of the night alone, and why I find you kissing my daughter, Carlton."

Mary snatched up the book on the nearby shelf, holding it against her breast as if it would somehow protect her. No amount of armor would protect them for what was to come.

"I wanted to read and so came down to the library to fetch a book. His grace was helping me decide."

Dale cleared his throat as both Peter and Lord Lancaster threw disbelieving looks at Mary.

The need to protect her roared inside of him and he found himself saying, "Actually, I have asked Mary to be my wife and she's agreed."

Mary let out a little yelp, but he didn't look at her. His lordship gaped at him, and Peter glared. "What have you done to my sister, Carlton?"

He'd never heard his friend speak to him with such deadly ire before, and he clamped his jaw shut. He wasn't a fool and he certainly wasn't going to tell anyone that he'd just shagged Mary within an inch of her life, and damn well enjoyed every delectable moment of it. The thought of marrying her should fill him with regret, with fear and yet it did not. She might test him at times, question his decisions, but surely, she would know how to conform to the role that was required of her as his wife. That he was a duke and she would need to be a true and elegant duchess. Perform her duties and not cause any trouble.

"Nothing, Peter," Mary said. She turned to him, clasping his arm. "Your grace, you do not need to offer simply because we were caught in the library together. A kiss is not such an offence that marriage is the outcome."

He took her hand, wrapping it into his, squeezing it a little when he noticed hers was shaking. "We will be married four weeks from now. The banns may be called. We'll marry here in the drawing room with only close family and friends. Are you in agreement, Lord Lancaster?"

Mary stared up at him, her eyes wide and filled with shock.

"Say yes," he said when she continued to stare at him as if he'd sprouted two heads. "Yes, Mary. Say it," he urged.

CHAPTER 13

*M*ary turned to her father. "May I have a moment with his grace, please, Papa? I need to speak to him about his proposal."

"Absolutely not," her brother interjected, slicing a finger through the air. "I think you've been alone quite enough already this evening."

Her father pursed his lips thinking over her request. "You may speak to the duke, but we shall be present. We will afford you a little privacy by going to stand before the fire."

Mary waited for her father and brother to move away, before she turned back to Dale, not quite sure how he could seem so calm and in control of himself. She was beyond confused and her heart seemed to be beating louder than a drum in her ears. "Why me, your grace?"

"What do you mean, why me?" He glanced at her clearly confused. "After what just happened, I thought you might be a little relieved rather than questioning my declaration."

Mary frowned, not wanting anyone to marry her out of obligation. "You know that I wanted to marry someone who, if at all possible, I loved. A man that would allow me to continue in the same vein in which I live now. To remain in the country instead of in Town. You, your grace cannot be that man."

He cleared his throat, and stood taller like a soldier as if he were about to go into battle. "I like you, I think that we will do well enough together. As for how you live, you must understand there will be limitations of course. I'm a duke, when you marry me you'll be a duchess. Your place will be at my side, having said that," he said at her gasp, "that does not mean that we'll always be in Town. We shall return to Carlton Hall regularly, and certainly often enough to sate your desire for the outdoors."

Mary stared at him a moment, lost for words. A week in Town was too much. London had always made her feel out of place. It was simply not who she was. If he forced her, their marriage would not be a happy one. "But that's not what I want. I don't want to be in London most of the time. I want to marry a man who suits me and my character, my likes and dislikes. You do not."

"We do suit. We suited very well not half an hour ago," he whispered.

At his scandalous reminder heat shot across her skin. "Hush, my father will hear. And you know that is not what I mean. If I have to marry, I want to marry a man who prefers the country to Town. You do not and your standing within the *ton* would mean that I would have to be by your side all the time. Never mind the fact that you do not want a wife. I fail to believe that all of a sudden you've had an epiphany and now want a wife."

"I have not had an epiphany, I'm merely doing what is right and you will marry me, Lady Mary. There is no choice. I think you understand as well as anyone the possible repercussions of our meeting earlier tonight."

Oh yes, she understood very well all the repercussions of

what had transpired between them. Of being forced into a marriage neither of them wanted, and the possibility that she might fall pregnant. "I'm too opinionated for you. If we were to marry, you would soon tire of me not wishing to follow you to London. I don't want to quarrel with you."

He blanched at the mention of such a thing, and ran a hand through his hair, leaving it on end. "We shall not quarrel if you behave like a duchess, the well-bred young woman that you are, we will get along well enough."

She raised her brows. "I'm not one to be told what to do, your grace." She took a step away, crossing her arms across her chest. "I will not marry you."

"You have no choice."

Mary swallowed the bile that rose in her throat. The thought of being a social matriarch, of hosting and giving balls and soirées left her dizzy with dread. She could not do it. "Everyone has a choice."

Dale turned back toward his lordship and Peter. "It is agreed. One month, my lord, and Lady Mary will be the new Duchess of Carlton."

Her father burst into a smile, clapping his hands. Her brother, however, stared at the duke with deadly ire.

"Congratulations, your grace. Mary darling." Her father shook Dale's hand and pulled Mary into an embrace.

"I wish to talk to the duke," Peter said, not using the duke's given name. An oddity, for Mary had only ever known her brother to use the duke's given name while at home these past weeks.

Her father readily agreed. "Of course. No doubt you wish to have a toast celebrating the newly engaged couple." He pulled Mary toward the hall. "Come, Mary. Tell me of your wishes for your wedding day." Mary glanced over her shoulder meeting Dale's gaze as they left, so much still left unsaid between them. Did he believe she would not marry him or did he truly think them engaged?

Her father walked her upstairs, discussing how happy this news would make her mother and her throat tightened with panic. This was exactly the situation in which she did not want to find herself and for all the duke's gentleman-like honor, it was not needed here. Not yet at least.

Her father stopped at her bedroom door. "We shall tell your mother together tomorrow. Now," he said, opening her door and ushering her inside. "Off to bed, my dear. The next few weeks will be busy indeed and you need your rest."

Mary stared at the door as it closed. Had they all lost their minds? What about what she wanted, what the duke wanted, what he really wanted. It was not her he really wanted, she was certain of that.

If there was one thing she disliked it was being managed, and she'd been utterly managed this evening. She stomped her foot, and growled at the door. It wasn't to be borne and she would not be marrying anyone unless he loved her enough to allow her to be who she was. *Always*. And it did not escape her that if he had offered a word of love…of some gesture, she would have said yes. The ache in her heart bloomed to encompass her entire body. How could she really consent to marry a man she feared she had fallen so much in love with…but he only *liked* her?

*D*ale turned back to Peter after losing sight of Mary and her father. She was shocked, there was no doubt, and probably felt a little managed by him as well. In time he hoped she would thaw to the idea. He was not the type of man to hold anyone back from being who they were, and he would not start now with his wife. Only in society would he expect Mary to abide by society's line.

She would have to be by his side when he went to London, for either the Season or when Parliament resumed, but when they were not obligated to be in Town, the idea of being carefree, home on his estate with Mary made him eager for the first time in as long as he could remember to go home.

He walked over to the decanter of whisky pouring both himself and Peter a glass. He held it out to his friend who followed him and placed it on the sideboard when he didn't venture to take it. "Say it," he said to Peter when he merely stood before him, glaring.

"How could you," Peter said, pointing a finger in his direction and stabbing it at him as if he wished it were a blade. "Did you ruin her? Could you not, out of respect for our friendship, not leave my sister alone. Do you not have enough women to warm your bed that you had to take an innocent, your best friend's sibling?"

Dale raised his chin, hating that Peter's words were true. All of them. He was a cad. Known about London for his many lovers, his wayward nights on the town. But Dale also could admit to himself that his lifestyle no longer satisfied. He was sick of it, weary of keeping up an appearance when in truth his desires had shifted.

Having Mary tonight had been the moment he realized she made him feel complete. Satisfied beyond measure. A niggling of it had occurred when in the linen closet, but being with her fully this evening had proven the point. As much as he'd railed about marriage, he was simply railing against the institution because he'd not found the right woman.

His parents' marriage had been a disaster because there were no feelings between them, other than annoyance and regret. He liked Mary at least, and she was an earl's daughter, not wholly wild at heart. That he'd ruined her came into play. She could be carrying his child, and that alone forced his hand into offering marriage.

"I will be faithful to Mary. You have my word on that. I like your sister very much and her exuberance. She will keep me on my toes." And it would be no hardship to have the little hellion in his bed at night.

Peter threw him a disbelieving look. "I find that hard to believe. You may have been one of my best friends, but should you hurt my sister in any way, I will make you pay."

"I shall not hurt her. On the contrary, I shall try and make her happy." Try and ensure that their home life was a happy one. A peaceful, calm place that they would never bicker in.

"You dislike confrontation, and Mary is the embodiment of all that. She is not a woman to be managed and if you try and force her you will find your marriage one of regret."

The pit of his gut clenched at the thought of having an unhappy marriage. Mary was independent and opinionated. A slither of doubt entered his mind that he'd been hasty in acting the gentleman. But then, being caught kissing after he'd shagged her forced his hand in any case.

"I know you, Carlton, and I know how you suffered in your parents' home. I do not want to find my sister has entered a similar fate as that of your mother."

Dale clenched his jaw. The insinuation from his friend hurt and he took a couple of moments to cool his temper. "I would never abuse Mary or any woman. How could you think I would?"

"I do not think you would, but she's my sister. My concern stands with her."

Dale stared at Peter as he stormed from the room. Damn it, he didn't want them to fall out over this. He'd broken Peter's trust to be sure, but he would do all that he could to make Mary happy. He might not love her, but many marriages had started out on less solid foundations and survived.

He drank down his whisky and then not wanting to waste the second glass that sat untouched on the sideboard, he drank that down too. All would be well, he was sure of it, and in time he would prove to Mary, Peter, everyone that their misgivings on the match were unfounded.

CHAPTER 14

One month later

Mary stared at herself in the mirror in her bedroom, a bride staring back at her. She took in the dark locks pulled into line by many pins and a pretty veil that sat over the top of her curls, lying softly over her silk and embroidered light blue gown.

After her marriage today she would be the Duchess of Carlton. She stared at herself, her eyes too large it would seem, a frightened tinge to their appearance.

Her stomach roiled at the thought of marrying the duke. She'd not seen him these past four weeks. He'd left Christmas Day after their betrothal announcement stating he needed to return to London to prepare for their marriage and to notify his many estates that they would visit each one during their honeymoon.

She clasped her hands, trying to ignore the excited chatter of her mama and Louise who were in the room with her.

"Mother, I need to see the duke. At once," she said, her voice but a whisper.

"What was that, my darling?" Her mama came over to her, her brow furrowed in concern.

"I need to speak with Dale. Before I marry him. I need to speak with him alone. I will not attend downstairs until I do."

Louise and her mama glanced at each other, a question in both their eyes. Mary took a calming breath, knowing it would not appear well that she was asking for such a thing, but she needed to speak with Dale. Needed to know before she took her vows that he would not expect her to be the perfect duchess that she could never be.

"I will go fetch him," her mama said. Louise came over and clasped her hand, squeezing it a little before too, leaving her alone. Mary went and sat on her bed, waiting for Dale. The heavy, determined footfalls sounded in the hall outside her door and her stomach fluttered knowing she'd see him again.

Her door opened and then he was there. The perfect, magnificent Duke of Carlton that made women's heads turn at every event. If she had to marry at all she could never share him, and to think that their marriage could end as so many *ton* marriages did, with disillusioned couples that tolerated each other but little else would not do for her.

She had never wanted to marry, but to marry without some sort of affection, without some sort of promise that he wouldn't box her into the life of a proper, respectable, biddable wife was no life at all. She'd rather be ruined than suffer such a fate.

*D*ale remembered to breathe as he looked upon Mary, whom oddly he'd missed the last month while away in Town. She was so beautiful, so different from the ribbon-and-lace wallflower that he'd met prior to Christmas.

The woman who sat before him was poised, elegant, a true duchess, but the glint of independence, or rebellion flickered in her green eyes and gave him pause.

"You look beautiful Mary," he said, coming over to her. She stood, meeting his gaze with an unflinching strength that he admired. "You wanted to see me?"

She clasped her hands before her, biting her lip and his body hardened at the sight. He'd missed her, not just her lively conversations and blunt, to the point opinions, but also he'd missed being with her. Alone.

"I wanted to talk to you about us. About what you expect from me as your wife."

Dale sat on the bed, pulling her down to do the same. He took her hand, unable to stop himself from rubbing his thumb across the inside of her wrist. His ministrations brought a delightful flush to her cheeks and all he wanted to do was to kiss her. To take her into his arms and prove to her, that whatever concerns she might have about them, they were not warranted.

Over the past month he'd reflected a lot on his life, on his parents' marriage. One thing was clear above all else. He was not his father, and Mary was not his mother. They had entered the marriage with no affection and as the years went by, their discontentment, their dislike of each other had turned toxic.

He was not that type of man. He would never be that kind of weak person who took out their frustrations, their rage on others.

"Go on. State your terms." He schooled his features, willing to give her anything that she wished so long as she was his by the end of the day.

She looked down at their entwined hands, her brow furrowed. "You know my character. You know that I'm independent and opinionated, and also a bit of a bluestocking. After having been caught in a compromising situation with you and seeing that there was no other option for us to marry, I do think that we'll do well enough as any other couple setting out on this marriage journey. But," she said, pausing.

He lifted her chin, needing to see her eyes. "But what, Mary?" he asked.

Her tongue darted out and licked her lips and Dale fought to concentrate on the conversation at hand. He was totally besotted by a woman that in truth he hardly knew. He wondered at the emotions roiling throughout him, what they meant before pushing them away to listen to what she had to say.

"But I will not change who I am to suit your friends, your title or your expectations of what you may think a duchess should be like. If I see or hear something that I think is cruel, or untrue I will seek to repair the error. I will not like people to further your standing in the *ton*, and I will not stop my hobbies. Any of them, even climbing rocky outcrops that I do most summers."

He bit back a bemused smile. She was perfect. "Is there anything else?" he asked, his tone severe.

Her eyes flared, but instead of crumbling under his supposed ire, she lifted her chin, her determination to get what she wanted overriding her fear of his opinion. "I will not share you, your grace. Not with anyone. Ever. If I ever heard word that you've been unfaithful to me, our marriage will be at an end. I may not be able to divorce you, but that is exactly what will happen without all the legalities of it. If I'm to be your wife, it is my bed and only my bed that you'll find yourself in. If you're unable to promise me my wishes, I will not marry you today."

*T*he duke stared at her, his face giving little away as to what he was thinking. His hand still held hers, his thumb making her insides quake with remembering how they were together when alone. How very clever his hands were when on her person.

She took a calming breath, waiting for him to speak. How had all her hopes ended up being tied to a man she knew very little beyond a month ago?

"They are a lot of stipulations." He stood, walking a few steps from her. His back was rigid, proud and Mary knew what she asked was a lot. Possibly too much for a man of his rank and power to allow. But she could not give herself over to anyone unless they allowed her to be who she was. A rough and tumble girl from Derbyshire who didn't play by the rules, and never wanted to.

"But I find myself at liberty to agree to your terms. I should not expect anything less from my duchess," he said, turning toward her, a wicked grin on his lips.

Mary let out a relieved sigh, standing and throwing herself into his arms. His arms came about her, strong and fierce and within a moment she found herself kissing him. Their lips entwined, his hands over her back, her bottom and then one thigh as he lifted her up against his heat.

She moaned, kissing him with a fierceness that left her breathless, very much looking forward to tonight when they were alone. The idea frightened and exhilarated her at the same time. Whatever the duke evoked in her was new and absolutely wonderful.

"Do you really mean it?" she asked, pulling back and wrapping her arms about his neck.

He nodded, his eyes dark with unsated need. "Oh yes, I mean it. I did not think I wanted a duchess, nor one that I knew would push and pull me in all directions, but that was until I found you. I will never hurt you. I shall never dishonor you. You have my word on that."

Mary smiled, her eyes smarting with tears. "I suppose we should go downstairs and get married then, your grace."

He lowered her to the ground, kissing her softly once more. A kiss that seemed filled with a promise of forever. "I suppose we should."

He stepped to her side, holding out his arm. "Shall we, Lady Mary?" he asked, the proper gentleman and duke once more.

Mary threaded hers arm through his, a rightness settling over her like a balm. "We shall."

EPILOGUE

Spring 1801 - The Season

*M*ary stood beside her husband whose hand lay gently on the arch of her back. His thumb brushed slowly back and forth, and she smiled, knowing he was teasing her on purpose.

"Behave," she said, smiling up at him.

He grinned back. "I do not know what you're talking about."

She shook her head, watching her friend Louise take part in a country dance, the first of many now that they were back in Town. It was bittersweet for Mary, as Louise would soon be off to York and no longer her companion. She would miss her friend dearly.

Mary watched with growing concern as Louise looked less than pleased to be in the arms of Lord Lindhurst. "She's not enjoying herself. She looks positively bored."

The duke cast a curious glance in Louise's direction, his lips thinning in agreement. "So it would seem." He paused, turning to look at Mary. "Are you sure she wants to go to

York. You have stressed that she's more than welcome to stay with us, have you not?"

Mary frowned, knowing it was what Louise wanted. "I will talk to her when we return home. Maybe I can convince her to stay."

The duke nodded, pulling her closer, his arm slipping about her waist to lay across the small bundle of life that grew within her belly. Their child. Just the thought of having a son or daughter left her overjoyed, and now that she was married to Dale, pregnant and utterly happy, she could not imagine her life any other way.

Dale had been true to his word. He'd taken her to all his estates during their wedding trip and she had explored his lands, ice fished when weather permitted and anything else that took her fancy. Not once had he tried to cut her wings, and now a new adventure grew within her, a lifetime of surprises and happy moments to come.

She could not wait.

"What are you thinking about?" he asked, meeting her eyes. "You have the oddest look upon your face."

Mary covered his hand on her waist with her own. "I'm just thinking about how happy I am. How happy you make me. This is terribly gauche of me, but I'm glad we were caught in the library that night. I thought what I had before was all that I wanted, but it was not. I was deluding myself."

He kissed her temple, ignoring the startled glances thrown their way at such a public show of affection. "Have I told you that I'm also glad of that night. Not simply because it was so very pleasurable," he whispered against her ear, making her chuckle. "But because it meant that I won you. I adore you," he said, tipping up her chin to look at him.

Mary stared at him a moment, having never heard him say such a sentimental thing before. "You do?"

He nodded, his eyes darkening in hunger. "I think it's

been quite obvious for a few months now, and I'm sure the *ton* knows as well that the Duke of Carlton has fallen in love with his wallflower bride."

Mary bit her lip, her eyes blurring with unshed tears. "You love me?" To hear him say such things made her heart want to burst from her chest. Relief poured through her, thankful that she was not the only one to suffer such a fate.

"I do. I think in fact that I fell in love with you the first moment I saw you in that ridiculous dress with all those ribbons and bows. You were the most adorable, unfortunate being, that how could one not possibly fall in love with such a woman."

She smacked his hand playfully before clasping it. "I suppose if we're being honest with each other I should tell you too, that I find myself of similar emotions to you, your grace?"

He looked at her skeptically. "Surely you can do better than that, duchess."

She turned into his arms, wrapping her hands about his neck. The duke held her close, unafraid to scandalize the *ton* that the Duke and Duchess of Carlton were being too forward in public. Mary played with the hair on his nape, watching him as he waited. "I love you too," she said, leaning up further and kissing him. "I think I fell in love with you the moment I felt your hard, delicious abdomen beneath my hands in the conservatory. How could a woman be immune to such a being?"

"You are truly too bold, duchess, but never change. Promise me you'll never stop being you."

Mary leaned up once again. "I can promise you that," she said, kissing him again, this time not stopping even when the gasps and some whistles from the gathered throng told them they should. Mary had never been one to conform to Society's rules, and she wasn't about to start now.

Dear Reader,

Thank you for taking the time to read *A Kiss at Mistletoe*! I hope you enjoyed the second book in my Kiss the Wallflower series. Mary and Dale were a fun pair to write, and who doesn't love a Christmas house party where scandal and secret kisses ensue.

I'm forever grateful to my readers, so if you're able, I would appreciate an honest review of *A Kiss at Mistletoe*. As they say, feed an author, leave a review! You can contact me at tamaragillauthor@gmail.com or sign up to my newsletter to keep up with my writing news.

If you'd like to learn about book three in my Kiss the Wallflower series, *A Kiss in Spring*, please read on. I have included chapter one for your reading pleasure.

Tamara Gill

A KISS IN SPRING

KISS THE WALLFLOWER, BOOK 3

A broken carriage wheel at the base of the Scottish highlands is the last thing Sophie Grant needs on her trip to Scotland. Determined to make the most of her stay in the quaint village of Moy, she discovers some delightful attractions, including the Laird Mackintosh, who lives nearby.

. . .

Upon an invitation to the Laird's home, Sophie is thrust into a world of decadence, privilege, and wealth—everything she never had. Laird Mackintosh is tempting and beguiling with his scandalously hot kisses. However, Sophie knows he's hiding something—something that could change everything.

Brice Mackintosh is torn between his family's expectations, and his newfound feelings for Sophie. What started out as a game, a distraction before he fills his obligations is turning into more. But when the truth surfaces, Brice worries that he may lose the only woman he's ever loved.

CHAPTER 1

Highlands Scotland 1805

Sophie Grant dozed halfway between asleep and awake as the carriage continued on north, heading toward a small fishing village near the Isle of Skye. She'd never been to Scotland before and after this arduous journey, she doubted she'd ever go again.

How far away could this little seaside village be? Even so, they'd been traveling for what felt like months, but was in fact only weeks. Granted, they had stopped most nights, and during some breaks, had extended the journey to take in the local attractions or simply to rest both themselves, their driver and the horses.

She settled back into the squabs, luxuriating in the plush velvet seats and highly polished equipage. At least her little sojourn was more comfortable than taking the post. Her new brother-in-law, the Marquess Graham had insisted she use one of his carriages and had sent both a coachman and manservant to ensure her and her maid's safety.

So far they had very little to complain about, except the

never-ending road or that the farther north they traveled the colder it seemed to get.

Sophie had thought spring in Scotland would be warmer than this, but apparently not.

A loud crack sounded and the carriage lurched frighteningly to one side. Sophie slipped off the seat and landed with a thump on the floor, her maid, sleeping on the opposite seat came crashing down on top of her and supplying Sophie with an elbow to the temple.

Distantly she could hear the coachman and manservant talking outdoors before the door swung open and the driver was there, taking in their disheveled appearance.

"Are you hurt, Miss Sophie, Miss May?" he asked, reaching in to help her maid climb off Sophie and regain her footing.

Sophie untangled herself from her dress and managed to slide toward the door and then step out onto the uneven, pothole-filled dirt road.

"Well, I think we can at least say why our wheel has broken in two." Sophie glanced at the sad wooden wheel lying beside the carriage, several spikes missing completely, possibly on the road behind them before the wheel collapsed under the carriage's weight.

"We're not far from the town Moy. I can leave you here with Thomas and go and fetch a new vehicle or we can all walk to town and I'll return later to pick up Thomas and collect your belongings."

"We'll walk with you, Peter. If you're happy to wait here with the carriage, Thomas?" Sophie asked, not wanting him to stay here alone if he did not feel comfortable.

"I'm armed, Miss Sophie. I'll wait here until Peter returns. Town is not so far away, I can see smoke from some chimneys already."

Sophie looked north up the road and true enough, there were little swirls of smoke floating up in the air behind a small rise in the road. "Oh, we're not far at all." She reached into the carriage and looked for her reticule. Finding it on the floor, she picked it up and turned back to their little group. "Shall we?"

The walk into the village took no longer than half an hour and soon enough they were walking past the few cottages the village sported. A small sign pronounced the town to be Moy. A few of the locals came out to stare and some welcomed them with a friendly smile or wave.

"Do you think there is an inn in town, Miss Sophie? That carriage wheel will take some days to repair," her maid, Gretel, asked, looking about the town with a less-than-pleased visage.

Sophie took account of the sleepy village, fear that there would be no inn washed over her. "I hope so. We need to secure rooms for some days and wait out the repairs. We're in no rush after all, and the carriage being Lord Graham's, I'd prefer to wait for it to be fixed than leave it here. But there doesn't seem to be a lot of people living here."

"I'm sure all will work out, Miss Sophie. Do not worry," Peter said, throwing her an easy smile.

They came to a crossroad and thankfully spied what looked like the local inn. It was made of stone and a thatch roof. A carriage sat parked to the side, and a young stable lad placed luggage at its back.

Sophie hoped that it was a place travelers could stay, or they would need to leave Marquess Graham's carriage here and travel on without it. If there was a carriage they could procure, in any case.

Peter led the way into the taproom, which had some men seated at the bar drinking ale. A barman with a long, graying beard came up to them and leaned upon the counter. "What can I help ye with?" he asked, taking each of them in before turning back to Peter.

"We're after two rooms if you have them available. Our carriage has broken a wheel outside of town and I'll need a cart to collect our luggage, if you please."

The barman rubbed his bearded jaw. "Ach, we can help ye with that to be sure, but I only have one room left, we're not officially an inn, but we can help ye out since our guests overnight are leaving as we speak. If you're willing, sir, I can put you up in the stables on a cot."

Peter nodded. "That will be fine. We'll need two cots as I have left a manservant with the carriage."

The barman stood, and Sophie found herself looking up at the towering gentleman. He was as tall as he was wide, his fiery-red hair and stature perfect for the position he held. "No trouble, sir, that can be arranged." He bellowed out for a woman named Bridget and within a minute a young woman bustled into the room, her hair askew and her apron covered in cooking stains. She smiled at each of them and Sophie smiled back.

"Show these ladies upstairs and have Alfie set up two cots in the stable. We'll also be needing the cart hitched."

"Of course, Father," she said, opening a small door in the bar and coming out to them. "If ye will follow me, my ladies. I'll show ye to your room."

"We'll be in the stable, Miss Sophie. I'll have Thomas bring in your luggage when we return with it."

"Thank you, Peter." Sophie followed the young woman up a narrow flight of stairs, stepping to the side when another young woman carrying a bucket and dressed in similar clothing to Bridget passed them on their way down.

They made their way along a passageway before coming to a room at the very end. The young woman unlocked the door with a key and swung it wide open.

"Here is ye room, my ladies. I'll have hot water and linens brought up straightaway. There is a private parlor downstairs if ye do not wish to eat in your lodgings, but ye do have a small table and two chairs if ye wish to."

Sophie walked into the room, taking in the double bed that looked clean and inviting. The curtains were new and there were flowers on a small table. A fire burned in the grate and the room was warm and welcoming.

"This is lovely," she said, stripping off her shawl and throwing it on the bed along with her reticule. "For an inn that doesn't trade in accommodation, it is very well-kept and presentable."

The young woman blushed at the compliment and her chin rose slightly with pride. "Aye, we're very lucky. The inn is owned by our local laird Brice Mackintosh but run by my father. His sister is responsible for the recent refurbishment of this room. 'Tis the only one we have since the building is so small. The few patrons we get here always appreciate a clean bed and good meal."

"That they do," Gretel said, sliding back the curtain to look outside. "May we order an early dinner? We've been traveling all day and I have to admit to being quite famished."

"Of course," the young woman said. "We're serving roast chicken and beef stew this evening, which do you prefer?"

At the mention of food Sophie's stomach rumbled. "I'll have the stew please, and a pot of tea if possible."

"I'll have the same, thank you," Gretel said, pulling off her shawl and laying it on a chair by the fire.

The young woman bobbed a quick curtsy and started for the door. "I'll be back shortly, my lady."

"You may call me Miss Grant."

"Aye, of course. I shall return, Miss Grant." The door closed behind the young woman and Sophie stripped off her gloves, placing them on the mantel as she warmed herself before the fire.

"What a lovely inn and so accommodating. Certainly a much more pleasant place than some of the English ones we've stayed in."

Gretel nodded, coming to sit at the small table. She pulled off her gloves before yawning. "I'm dreadfully tired. A nice meal will be just what we need, along with a good night's rest."

The warmth from the fire slowly penetrated Sophie's bones and she shut her eyes, reveling in being warm and out of the jarring carriage. "I think we'll be here for several days. Perhaps there is a carriage-maker in the town who can repair the wheel, but I'm doubtful. I should say it will have to be brought up with the post from London."

"But that could take weeks," Gretel said, her eyes wide with alarm. "Although the lodgings are very comfortable, whatever will we do for all that time? Is there anything about to look at? I think I could count on one hand how many cottages were here."

Sophie walked to the window and stared out at the street, spotting a blacksmith and a small shop of some kind, but from where she stood she couldn't make it out.

"We'll ask tomorrow what there is to see and do here. I'm sure we can pass the time well enough, and anyway, we've been on the road for so long, a little break from travel will do us good."

Gretel nodded. "I'm sure you're right."

A light knock sounded on the door before it opened and Bridget entered, carrying a tray of tea and biscuits, along with a small bowl of cream and jam. She placed it down on the table. "The tea has just been poured, so perhaps let it sit for a little while before taking a cup."

"Thank you, it looks delicious."

"I'll bring dinner up in about ten minutes. Cook is just finishing it up now."

Sophie smiled at her, seating herself at the table. "Thank you, that is very good of you."

"You're welcome, Miss Grant."

When they were alone once again, Gretel went about putting cream and jam onto the biscuits along with preparing the tea for them to drink. They sat in silence for a time as they ate and enjoyed the refreshing drink, both lost in their thoughts.

"The young woman said that the inn is owned by the local laird and his sister. Perhaps we can visit with them. I've never met a Scottish laird before. He may live in a castle," Sophie teased. "I know how much you enjoy old houses."

Gretel nodded as she took a rather large bite of her biscuit. "I've always thought that Scottish lairds lived in castles, so I would expect nothing else," she mumbled.

Sophie chuckled. "I think I understood what you said, but really, Gretel, maybe smaller bites in the future."

Gretel smiled, her eyes bright with laughter. "Of course," she mumbled yet again.

Sophie poured herself another cup of tea. Being stuck in this sleepy but quaint town would surely be diverting enough to while away their time until the carriage was repaired. The landscape alone was beautiful, the forest and surrounding rugged hills drew the eye and beckoned one to explore. Maybe if they hired a local guide, they could picnic at a location the locals enjoyed.

Yes, they could have ended up stranded in much worse locations than Moy and they would make the best of their time while they were here.

LORDS OF LONDON SERIES
AVAILABLE NOW!

Dive into these charming historical romances! In this six-book series by Tamara Gill, Darcy seduces a virginal duke, Cecilia's world collides with a roguish marquess, Katherine strikes a deal with an unlucky earl and Lizzy sets out to conquer a very wicked Viscount. These stories plus more adventures in the Lords of London series!

LEAGUE OF UNWEDDABLE GENTLEMEN SERIES AVAILABLE NOW!

Fall into my latest series, where the heroines have to fight for what they want, both regarding their life and love. And where the heroes may be unweddable to begin with, that is until they meet the women who'll change their fate. The League of Unweddable Gentlemen series is available now!

LEAGUE OF UNWEDDABLE GENTLEMEN

TO VEX A VISCOUNT

TO DARE A DUCHESS

TO MARRY A MARCHIONESS

LORDS OF LONDON - BOOKS 1-3 BUNDLE

LORDS OF LONDON - BOOKS 4-6 BUNDLE

To Marry a Rogue Series

ONLY AN EARL WILL DO

ONLY A DUKE WILL DO

ONLY A VISCOUNT WILL DO

ONLY A MARQUESS WILL DO

ONLY A LADY WILL DO

A Time Traveler's Highland Love Series

TO CONQUER A SCOT

TO SAVE A SAVAGE SCOT

TO WIN A HIGHLAND SCOT

Time Travel Romance

DEFIANT SURRENDER

A STOLEN SEASON

Scandalous London Series

A GENTLEMAN'S PROMISE

A CAPTAIN'S ORDER

A MARRIAGE MADE IN MAYFAIR

SCANDALOUS LONDON - BOOKS 1-3 BUNDLE

High Seas & High Stakes Series

HIS LADY SMUGGLER

HER GENTLEMAN PIRATE

HIGH SEAS & HIGH STAKES - BOOKS 1-2 BUNDLE

Daughters Of The Gods Series
BANISHED-GUARDIAN-FALLEN
DAUGHTERS OF THE GODS - BOOKS 1-3 BUNDLE

Stand Alone Books
TO SIN WITH SCANDAL
OUTLAWS

ABOUT THE AUTHOR

Tamara is an Australian author who grew up in an old mining town in country South Australia, where her love of history was founded. So much so, she made her darling husband travel to the UK for their honeymoon, where she dragged him from one historical monument and castle to another.

A mother of three, her two little gentlemen in the making, a future lady (she hopes) and a part-time job keep her busy in the real world, but whenever she gets a moment's peace she loves to write romance novels in an array of genres, including regency, medieval and time travel.

www.tamaragill.com
tamaragillauthor@gmail.com

Made in the USA
Coppell, TX
08 August 2021